Edith Herself

to Mrs. McFadyen's Class,
themselves!

Ellen Howard
1994

Ellen Howard

Edith Herself

illustrated by Ronald Himler

A JEAN KARL BOOK

ALADDIN BOOKS
Macmillan Publishing Company · *New York*

Maxwell Macmillan Canada · *Toronto*

Maxwell Macmillan International
New York · Oxford · Singapore · Sydney

First Aladdin Books edition 1994
Text copyright © 1987 by Ellen Howard
Illustrations copyright © 1987 by Ronald Himler

Aladdin Books
Macmillan Publishing Company
866 Third Avenue
New York, NY 10022

Maxwell Macmillan Canada, Inc.
1200 Eglinton Avenue East
Suite 200
Don Mills, Ontario M3C 3N1

Macmillan Publishing Company is part of the Maxwell Communication
Group of Companies.

Printed in the United States of America
10 9 8 7 6 5 4 3 2 1

A hardcover edition of Edith Herself is available from Atheneum,
Macmillan Publishing Company.

Library of Congress Cataloging-in-Publication Data

Howard, Ellen.
Edith herself / Ellen Howard. — 1st Aladdin Books ed.
p.   cm.
Summary: Orphaned by her mother's death, Edith goes to live with
her older sister and her dour husband in their stern Christian
farming household, where the strain of adjusting seems to aggravate
her epileptic seizures.
ISBN 0-689-71795-4
[1. Epilepsy—Fiction.   2. Farm life—Fiction.   3. Orphans—
Fiction.]   I. Title.
PZ7.H83274Ed   1994
[Fic]—dc20   93-28061

In memory of

GRANNY

Edith Del Rohrbough Slate
April 2, 1888–August 3, 1967

She taught me the things
I value most: story and family.

CONTENTS

Ring-a-ring o' roses,
A pocket full of posies,
A-tishoo! A-tishoo!
We all fall down.

The cows are in the meadow
Lying fast asleep,
A-tishoo! A-tishoo!
We all get up again.

—*The Oxford Dictionary of Nursery Rhymes*

Edith Herself

1
The Garden Alone

EDITH could hear them calling her.

Will's voice came from the barnyard—deep, and a little angry, she thought. She could hear his boots thud across the hard-packed ground, and she knew his hand was cupped to his mouth as he called, "Edith. Edith! You come on in now, you hear?"

Faith was on the front porch. Edith could hear the worry in her voice, and the worry pulled at Edith.

I should go in, Edith thought. But she didn't move. She crouched under the back steps, arms clasped around her knees and head bowed forward to make herself smaller, and she swayed, rocking herself back and forth as Mother used to rock her before Mother got sick. I should go in, Edith thought. Will'll give me a lickin', and Faithie'll cry again if I don't go in soon. But her body would not uncurl itself. There in the cool, damp, dog-smelling darkness of under-the-steps, clutching herself tight, Edith could keep the blackness in her head at bay.

It was safe under-the-steps. Here, no one spoke crossly to her or told her to get out from underfoot. They did not say, "Go play," to her as they dashed about doing scary, important things—things to do with Mother and sickness and the bad smells and dreadful sounds that came from Mother's room. They did not say, "Can't you see I'm busy?" or "Not now, Edie. Later. Maybe later. Go play." Yet under-the-steps, she could listen to them. She could feel them near and hear if something bad was going to happen, and if it did, she could curl herself more tightly into herself and shut her eyes and think of other things—nice things. Nothing bad could get her here under-the-steps, and the blackness in her head stayed away.

I should go in, Edith thought, but instead she began to sing softly to herself. "*I come to the garden alone,*" she sang and imagined the garden. It was her very own garden, she thought, full of all the flowers she loved—violets and pansies and forget-me-nots—all the small, shy flowers that grew in sheltered places. And roses too, of course, for that was what the song said: "*While the dew is still on the roses*"—little pink rosebuds, sweet and curled small—"*and the voice I hear, falling on my ear, the Son of God discloses. . . .*" Edith's voice rose, and she took a breath, imagining Him. She could see His eyes, blue like Mother's eyes, and they looked at her with love. "*And He walks with me, and He talks with me, and He tells me I am His own, and the joy we share . . .*"

"Edie, is that you?"

Edith swallowed her song. Her heart stopped. She held her breath and ceased rocking—listening, still.

"Edie? Are you under there?"

Edith felt the blackness creeping into her head. She exhaled a long whimpering breath.

Alena was crawling under the steps, her long skirts gathered over one arm. "Edie-love. Edie," she crooned. "Whatcha doin' under here? Are you hiding, Baby Sister? Are you hiding from us?"

Edith felt Alena's arms go around her. She smelled the clean, starchy smell of Alena's shirtwaist and a faint, homey odor of sweat and cooking and lavender water. Alena pulled her close and wriggled around in the darkness under-the-steps to find a comfortable place to rest her back.

"Say," said Alena, "it's nice under here in your hidey-hole. Nice and cool and safe. No wonder you like it."

Edith could hear the catch in Alena's voice—the strange, quivering, on-the-edge sound of the words. She put up her hand and touched Alena's face and felt the wet on her cheek. Alena was crying.

How strange that the blackness fled from her head the moment Edith knew for sure that the bad thing had happened at last. With her hand against Alena's wet cheek, Edith did not even have to hear her say it to know that Mother was dead.

Alena began to rock Edith in her arms. "What were you singing, Edie-love? What were you singing just now?" she asked, the sadness brimming in her voice.

And Edith began to sing again, softly, under her breath until Alena joined in. "*And the joy we*

*share as we tarry there, None other has ever
known."*

I T W A S decided when Alena's husband, John, came
to call the evening before the funeral. Edith heard
John talking to her older brothers and sisters. She
and her youngest brother, Chester, had been sent to
bed after family devotions, but they had not stayed
in bed.

"We ain't babies," Chester had said. "We got a
right to know. It's *us* they're decidin' about."

And so Edith and Chester had crept halfway
down the stairs and huddled there, where the voices
floated up to them from the sitting room.

"William and I can manage," Edith heard
Faith's voice ring out, unnaturally loud and bright.
"Don't worry about us."

"I need the boys to help out around the place,"
Will said. "We'll get along just fine."

"But Chessie's so young. . . ." came Alena's
worried voice.

"Not too young to help out," said Will, and
Edith felt the way Chester, on the step beside her,
straightened and squared his shoulders.

"I can help Will around the place," he whispered to Edith. "I'm plenty big to help."

"So can I," hissed Edith. "I can help."

"At least let us take Edie," she heard Alena say. "Edie would be company for Vernon. They're of an age."

Edith held her breath, listening hard. The silence from the sitting room stretched on and on.

"Well . . ." she heard Faith say at last.

"She would be welcome," John said, but Edith thought she heard something grudging in his voice.

"If you're sure . . ." said Will.

"You know we'd *love* to have her," Alena said. "I can mother her along with my own."

"Well . . . I suppose it might be best," Edith heard Faith say.

Something throbbed, hurting, in Edith's throat. She tucked her toes inside her nightgown and hugged herself.

"Then it's settled," she heard Alena say. "John and I will take Edie home with us."

"For a little while at least," said Faith. "Until we're settled."

"Yes," said Alena. "Yes, of course."

Edith thought that Chester was looking at her queerly—like he was measuring her.

"I get to go home with Alena," Edith said. "Alena wants *me*."

"Uh-huh," said Chester. "C'mon, we'd better go up before they catch us."

Edith followed Chester up the stairs. They crept along the edge next to the wall, where the treads didn't creak. Her heart was thudding hollowly in her chest. *Alena* wants me, she told herself, but her chin was trembling. Not to live at home anymore with Will and Faith and the boys! But Alena *wants* me, she told herself as she crawled between the sheets. She tried to imagine sleeping in a strange bed. Living in a strange house. Living with Alena . . . and John.

At the other end of the attic room, she could hear Chester rustling in his bed. " 'Night, Edie," Chester whispered.

" 'Night," Edith said and was proud her voice didn't betray the tears that were beginning to leak from beneath her tight-squeezed lids.

2
Home With Alena

THE AIR was stifling, even in the shade of the cemetery elms. Edith peeped from behind Alena's black skirts to watch all the black-clad women fan their shining faces with round paper fans. She watched the stiffly suited men shift from foot to foot and heard the uncomfortable creaking of their shoes. She heard Alena's baby whimpering in Alena's arms, just above her head. Edith clung to a fold of Alena's skirt and closed her eyes to shut out the frowning face of Alena's boy, Vernon. Above them towered John, making a long dark shadow that blocked the sun.

" 'Who can find a virtuous woman?' " Pastor Rost intoned. " 'For her price is far above rubies. . . .' "

Someone sobbed, and Edith opened her eyes and searched the assembled people for her brothers and her other big sister. There, there they were, quite near. Will had his arm around Faith—it was Faithie who had sobbed—and Chester and the other boys leaned against one another like stalks of corn in a sheaf, their towheads bent. Only sister Alena's family stood separate and erect, John setting the pattern with his eyes straight forward and his big white hands inflexibly at his sides.

Edith hung on tightly to Alena's skirt, feeling the warmth of Alena's body beneath it. She gazed up into Alena's set face. The tears were sliding silently from Alena's staring eyes. They fell on the baby in her arms.

" 'She girdeth her loins with strength, and strengtheneth her arms,' " Pastor Rost read. He was reading from the Bible, Edith knew. John had read

from the Bible, too, when he came to call last evening. He had said Mother was in Heaven with Father now, and ever since, Edith had been thinking
about that. Edith couldn't remember her father, but
if Heaven was anything like the Bible, Edith didn't
think Mother would like it much, for Bible stories
were confusing and strange—with very long old-
fashioned words—not like the fairy tales Mother
liked to tell that were clear and true, and funny
sometimes. It worried Edith a little that Mother
might be in Heaven, as John had said, but she
thought it more likely she had gone to Fairyland.

" '... her candle goeth not out by night,' " read
the pastor. Now *that* was more like Mother, Edith
thought and wondered to find that there was, after
all, something about Mother in the Bible. She listened carefully. " 'Strength and honour are her
clothing; and she shall rejoice in time to come.' "

"*And the joy we share as we tarry there, None
other has ever known,*" Edith hummed softly, and
little by little her sweaty fingers unclutched the
crumpled fold of Alena's black skirt.

Vernon was squirming. John quelled him with
a look and reached into his pocket for a handkerchief. Edith saw John give the handkerchief to
Alena. Then John reached out and took the baby.
Edith could feel Alena sway as the weight of the

baby was lifted from her arms. For a moment, she thought Alena was going to fall down, but then she felt her pull herself erect.

"Let us pray," the pastor said.

Edith saw Alena bow her head and wipe her eyes and blow her nose.

"The Lord lift up His countenance upon thee," Pastor Rost intoned, "and give thee peace."

"Amen," said the people.

"Amen," said Alena in a whisper.

"Amen," said John, his voice loud and firm.

Vernon was glaring at Edith, who had not bowed her head. "Amen," he said.

Edith blushed and bowed her head too late. "Amen," she whispered and stared in confusion at her feet.

The people began to move away from the hole in the ground where they had put the coffin. They turned to one another, clasping hands and shaking heads.

Suddenly, feeling the coldness of it in her toes and fingers, Edith realized Mother was in that coffin. They had put Mother in the coffin, not in Fairyland, and now two men were shoveling the mound of dirt beside the hole in on top of it. Edith could hear the dirt rattling on the coffin lid. She shuddered, frozen by the sound, and put her hands over her ears to shut it out. The blackness was crowding into her head.

Then Alena took her hand from her ear and held it, squeezing it softly as they walked away over the uneven ground. Edith was glad to be turned away from the hole in the ground, away from the rattling sound.

She heard John's big voice speaking firmly. "It is time to go home," he said.

THE SURREY came to a halt before John-and-Alena's house, and John helped Alena climb down. Edith thought Alena must have forgotten her, for she started toward the house without her. A screen door slammed, and an old man hurried out of the house. Edith saw him speak to Alena, and then Alena turned back toward the surrey, and Edith saw her look at them in a vague, distracted way. The old man put his arms around Alena and turned her again toward the house. He gave her a gentle shove.

John was lifting Vernon, cranky and whining, out of the surrey. Vernon's face was marked with the angry red circles the upholstery buttons had impressed on it as he slept during the drive.

"I'll take him, John," the old man said. "You bring the baby, and we'll get Alena's grip in a minute. It won't hurt the horses to stand."

"We've got another one, Father," John said.

Edith knew he meant her. She peered over the side of the surrey at the old man. He was big and rosy-looking, she saw, like Saint Nicholas, with his halo of gray hair and his full gray beard. Edith wondered if he were jolly, or stern like John, who never smiled at her. She watched him narrowly.

"Why, it's Edith!" the old man cried.

Edith flinched. The old man had a big loud voice like John's. She followed John with her eyes as he started toward the house, carrying Vernon.

"Bring her and the baby, will you, Father?" John asked.

Edith wondered. John called the old man Father. It seemed strange for a grown-up person like John to have a father, but then, Alena was grown-up, and Alena had a mother, the very same mother as Edith. . . . Edith's chin began to wobble, and she felt the empty, scary blackness rising up inside her.

"I'll not hurt you, child," the old man said, and this time his voice sounded gentle. "Come, let me help you down."

She slid across the seat obediently and held out her arms to him. He lifted her out of the surrey, and Edith liked the way his hands felt, strong and warm beneath her arms. He stood her on her feet, and she stared up at him as he lifted the baby's basket out of the surrey.

That's my little niece, that baby is, Edith thought. She liked thinking of it. It made her feel bigger and stronger. It was not so easy to imagine that Vernon was her nephew, he was so near her own age, but Alena had said it was so. "I'm your Aunt Edith," Edith had told Vernon before the funeral, but perhaps Vernon did not like aunts. He certainly hadn't been nice to *her*. And now she was to live with him at John-and-Alena's house.

"Edie would be company for Vernon," Alena had said.

And later, John had told Edith, "You can make yourself useful about the house." She would be living with John, too. . . .

Edith felt the blackness again. The old man took her hand. She concentrated on the feeling of his large warm hand holding hers, and the blackness ebbed away as he led her toward the house.

"Here we are," the old man said. "What shall we do with *this* young'un?"

Edith stopped shyly just inside the door, pulling her hand free from his. She waited to hear what Alena would say, but Alena only looked at her sadly and then turned her eyes to the old man.

"I wisht I could've come to the funeral, 'Lena," he said, putting the baby's basket on a chair. "I'm that sorry about your ma. She was a fine Christian woman. But Missus took a turn in the night, and I couldn't leave 'er. I'm that sorry. Was they a big crowd?"

"Yes," Alena said. "Yes, lots of folks. We were to have supper . . . afterwards. Everyone brought food. . . ."

"We didn't stay," John said. "Alena is worn out."

"I don't know what folks will think," Alena said, staring at a cup in her hands.

"It doesn't matter what folks think," John said. "The children were cross, and you needed to get home."

Edith frowned at John. I wasn't either cross, she thought.

"Home?" Alena was saying. "But I should have stayed to help. . . ."

"There were others to help. You have done enough, neglecting your own family to nurse your mother all these weeks."

"But it was my place. . . ."

"It was time to come home," John said, and the way he said it made Edith tremble.

"Yes," Alena said, and Edith saw tears well up in her eyes.

Edith edged around the kitchen wall toward the table where Alena sat. She crept to Alena's chair and laid her head against her sister's shoulder. Alena put an arm around her and gave her a squeeze, turning her face from John as the tears spilled over.

"I'll see to the horses," the old man muttered, and Edith saw him back out the door they had come in.

"Let's get this hat off," Alena said and pulled Edith in front of her. She unpinned the ill-fitting borrowed black hat. "I think you need a nap," she said.

John had gone to the drain board to pour himself a glass of water from the pitcher standing there. Edith watched him from the corner of her eye as Alena smoothed her hair and straightened her collar. Alena put her wet face against Edith's cheek.

"That's enough, Alena," John said sharply, and Edith jumped at the sound of his voice. "Don't fuss over the child," John said.

Edith saw Vernon had come to stand in a doorway across the room. He was dressed now in a pair of clean patched overalls. He looked cool and comfortable changed out of his hot woolen suit. Vernon glared at Edith. He thrust out his lower lip and drew his brows together. Edith saw his fists clench at his sides.

Alena had also jumped when John had spoken. She held Edith's hand tightly and looked at her husband. Then, slowly, her eyes unfocused, and her gaze dropped to her lap.

"Yes, John," Edith heard her say, and Alena let go of Edith's hand.

3

Belongings

AT HOME, some things had belonged to Edith. She
had her own end of the attic, partitioned from Chester's by a blue-gray curtain patterned with stars.
She had her own small cot beneath the eaves and her
own knitted afghan of dusty rose. She had a shelf

for her treasures and a chest for her clothes and a hook where she hung her coat.

At home, Edith had under-the-steps, her very own place, where no one came but her and Snitz. Snitz liked to crawl under-the-steps with Edith. He liked to pant his warm doggy breath in her face and thump his tail when she talked to him. He liked to lay his big heavy head in her lap while she scratched his ears. Just like he was *mine*, Edith thought.

At home, Edith had her own place at the table and her very own chair. It was the old high chair with the legs cut down. "The baby chair," teased Chester, " 'cause Edie is the baby."

But Edith didn't mind the teasing much. Sometimes being the baby was kind of nice. "Let Edie go first," they would say when it was a treat. "She's the baby." And when it was something hard, "Let Edie go last, and help her."

"My baby," Mother used to say with a special light in her eyes, and Edith knew that was what she missed most. At home, there had always been Mother. *My* mother, Edith thought. My very own.

At John-and-Alena's house, nothing belonged to Edith. "She can sleep on the daybed in the baby's room," Alena said. "She can use my sky blue quilt." Alena moved some of the baby's clothes to make room for Edith's. "You may put your other things in this," Alena said, giving her a small wooden crate. But Edith had nothing to put in the crate.

When Faith had packed her clothes the day of the funeral, she had not packed Edith's treasures. "You can get your other things later," Faith had said, but she had not said when "later" would be. Edith put her shoes into the crate when she went to bed.

One evening, she picked an aster growing under the white-oak tree. It seemed to Edith that she held in her hand a piece of the sky with a yellow moon at its center. When bedtime came, she put the aster into the crate beside her shoes. This piece-of-sky is mine, thought Edith. But in the morning, the flower was limp and colorless. I should have put it in water, Edith thought, and she threw it out the window. When she had hooked on her shoes, the crate was empty again.

All week at John-and-Alena's house, Edith looked for a place of her own. The veranda and porch were latticed to the ground. Vernon's Grandma Malcolm kept the keys on a ring at her waist, and even Alena had to ask permission to go into the pantry and the cellar. The upstairs belonged to Vernon.

Vernon's Grandpa Malcolm put the dictionary

on a kitchen chair for Edith. "She can sit here beside me," Alena said, but Vernon pouted.

"I *always* sit next to you, Mama," he whined. So John moved the chair with the dictionary to the other side of the table, next to Grandma Malcolm's chair. "I *always* sit next to my mama," Vernon said.

And Edith didn't say anything.

"You are a good big girl," Alena told her, while in her arms she nursed her own little baby.

AT CHURCH the next Sunday, Edith twisted in the slippery pew, watching for Faith and the boys.

"Sit up straight, Edith," John said, "and fold your hands in your lap. This is the House of the Lord."

Edith ducked her head, her cheeks going hot. Self-consciously, she folded her hands. She could feel Alena stiffen and hear the little protesting sound Alena made in her throat. She imagined Vernon was grinning. He held his back straight and stiff.

Then, from a corner of her eye, Edith caught sight of Faith's navy serge skirt swaying up the aisle toward the Ostermann family pew. Behind Faith marched Will and the boys. Edith let only her eyes move, watching as her sister and brothers filed into the pew on the other side of the church. Her heart was skipping joyfully. It seemed so long since she had seen them—last Sunday at the funeral. She longed to jump up and run to them, run to her place at the far end of the pew between Faith and . . . Mother. . . .

Edith's heart sank. Beside Faith's small blue hat rose Will's brown head and broad shoulders. Then Chester's, then Samuel's, then Delbert's, then Fritz's. There was no place there for Edith.

"ALENA Alena Malcolm!" Someone was calling behind them as they made their way up the aisle after the service. Edith looked over her shoulder and saw Mrs. Runyon bearing down upon them, the plumes of her velvet hat fluttering alarmingly.

Alena turned and held out her hand. "Mrs. Runyon," she said. "Good morning."

Mrs. Runyon hurried to them, her breath coming in little gasps. She shifted the brown-paper-wrapped parcel she held and clasped Alena's hand. "I didn't have a chance at the funeral, my dear, to tell you how very sorry I am about your mother."

Edith slipped behind Alena's skirts, almost colliding with Vernon. She did not want to hear what Mrs. Runyon was saying. She wanted to go find

Faith, as they had been about to do when Mrs. Runyon called.

Vernon stuck out his tongue. "Clumsy," he said.

"Am not," said Edith and looked for Faith. She had been standing near the doorway a moment ago, waiting for them. But now Edith could not see over the people crowding past them in the aisle. Many of the ladies were stopping to join Mrs. Runyon as she spoke to Alena about the funeral last Sunday.

"You slipped away so sudden." Mrs. Runyon's voice carried accusingly over the murmurs of the other ladies. "We hoped you wasn't ill."

Edith felt the long swaying skirts of the ladies press about her. The close, hot air laden with eau de cologne and the sharp, sour smell of the ladies' damp underarms was difficult to breathe. A plump, moist hand patted her head.

"Poor little orphan," Edith heard someone say.

Edith's heart was beginning to race. Her head felt light and, at the edges of her vision, darkness pressed. She tugged on Alena's skirt. " 'Lena," she said. " 'Lena. 'Lena!"

But Alena was caught in the strong web of Mrs. Runyon's voice. Edith glimpsed Alena's white face and the distracted glitter of her eyes.

Something was pulling at Edith, pulling on her

arm. She tried to shake it away. She twisted and looked into Vernon's exasperated face.

"C'mon, stupid," he said. "You're gonna get squashed."

Uncomprehending, Edith let him pull her out of the aisle and into the nearest pew.

"Old biddies!" Vernon muttered as he climbed up on the seat.

Edith stared at him, shocked. Why was Vernon angry all the time? She took a deep shaky breath and steadied herself against the back of the pew in front of them.

". . . as deserving as any little orphan in China . . ." Mrs. Runyon's voice was proclaiming. "Charity begins at home. . . . Mission Society wants her to have one. . . . Poor little Edith . . ."

"Edith."

"Edith Ostermann."

"Where has she got to?"

"Edith!"

"Oh, here she is!"

Hands were reaching for Edith. Once again she was being pulled, patted, touched.

Edith glanced wildly at Vernon. He was gazing at her, his face sullen and unreadable.

"Edie-love," Alena was saying. "Look what

Mrs. Runyon has for you. A present. A present from the Mission Society ladies."

Edith blinked. The hands had stopped tugging at her. The ladies stepped back, leaving a small space around her. Mrs. Runyon leaned forward, holding out the brown-paper-wrapped parcel. Her eyes were small and critical and did not match her wide benevolent smile.

"To comfort you in your grief, little dear," Mrs. Runyon said, and Edith was distressed to feel the eyes of all the ladies fixed on her.

What have I done? Edith thought. Why are they looking at me? She sought Alena's eyes.

"It's for you, Edie," Alena said. "It's a present for you."

Mrs. Runyon was thrusting the parcel into her hands.

"For me?" Edith whispered.

"Open it, little dear," Mrs. Runyon commanded, and Edith's fingers fumbled obediently at the string.

Edith could feel how hot and red her face was. Her hands shook, and the knot in the string pulled tighter.

"Here, Edie, let me help," came Faith's voice, and Edith looked up gratefully into Faith's blue eyes, their sympathy magnified behind her spectacles.

"Faithie!" Edith cried and would have dropped the parcel, forgotten, had not Faith rescued it and held it between them as Edith flung her arms around Faith's neck.

Faith answered Edith's hug and, keeping her within the circle of her arm, perched on the end of the nearest pew while her swift fingers sorted out the knotted string on the brown-paper parcel. Edith saw Vernon kneeling on the seat behind them, looking over Faith's shoulder.

"There you go, Edie," Faith said. "Now you can open it."

Edith unfolded the brown paper.

"Just a doll!" Vernon said. She felt him turn away.

Edith looked at the doll lying on Faith's knee. It was dressed in pink calico, bonnet and frock, with yellow curls peeping from beneath the bonnet's brim. Its embroidered blue eyes and rosy pink mouth smiled at her.

"For me?" Edith marveled aloud, touching a curl with a tentative finger.

Faith laughed and put the doll in Edie's arms.

"For you, Edie-love," Alena said, smiling.

"From the ladies of the Missionary Society. Can you say thank you?"

Edith could not take her eyes from the doll cradled in her arms. She squeezed the softness of its rag-stuffed body against her chest and laid her cheek against the bonneted top of its head. "My very own doll?" Edith whispered. She had never had a new doll of her own—only Faith's old one-armed baby with the smudgy face and corncob dollies made and discarded each harvest-time.

"Your very own," Faith said, and the ladies smiled and murmured.

Edith looked up. Mrs. Runyon's smile was growing thin and strained about the edges. Her sharp eyes pricked Edith.

"Thank you very much," Edith said quickly and loudly. She clutched the doll tightly to her chest so Mrs. Runyon could not snatch it away again.

4

Tug-o'-War

EDITH wandered across the yard, scuffling the dust with the toes of her shoes. She wished she had brought out her doll, but Pansy Violet Rosebud— for that was what she had named her—was taking a nap on the daybed. Edith's feet were hot. She thought of going back to the house to ask Alena if she could go barefooted—and to see if Pansy Violet Rosebud might have awakened by now—but Vernon was still on the back porch playing with the puppy.

"This is *my* dog," he had said. "My father gave him to me, and I say leave him alone."

"I just want to pet him."

"Well, he's *my* dog, and I say no."

She had stood, watching him. He was tickling the puppy's stomach while its legs waved in the air. When he drew back his hand, the puppy scrambled to its feet, bounced backward, yelping, and then lunged forward to lick Vernon's hand with a wet pink tongue while its tail thumped against the floor.

"That's not much of an ol' dog anyways," Edith had said. "My dog to home, now *there's* a dog. He don't like to play with nobody but me, Snitz don't. And *he's* big, the biggest dog in the world, I reckon."

"Not so big as Mr. Lewis's big ol' shepherd dog," said Vernon.

"Is too," Edith said, though she did not know Mr. Lewis or his dog. "He's bigger."

"Is not."

"Is too."

"Is not," Vernon said. " 'Sides, Snitz ain't *your* dog. He's Uncle William's dog. I heard Mama say so—said Uncle Will bought him off a man down to

Carthage for a dollar and a half. And Papa said it was a 'stravagance. So there!"

Edith felt a lump come into her throat. She knew if she said anything more, she would begin to cry, and then Vernon would call her an "ol' crybaby girl." She had turned on her heel, braids swinging out behind her, and flounced down the steps. She skipped halfway across the yard—skipping to show that she didn't care—before she turned to look back at him. He was crouched on his knees, absorbed in a game of tug-o'-war with the puppy over a piece of rope. So she wandered on, kicking at the dust and glancing back at the house from time to time. No, she would not go back just yet.

The sun was hot on the top of her head. The hot dust of the barnyard choked her nostrils. The orchard looked cool, but perhaps there were cows in the orchard. Edith was afraid of cows. She looked toward the grape arbor. They had been forbidden to play there afternoons while Vernon's Grandma Malcolm napped. It was too near her open window.

Edith leaned against the pigpen fence and looked in at the pigs. They were stretched out in the dust in the shade of the barn, snuffling now and then in their sleep. She watched the flickering of their ears and the way their skins jerked when flies landed on them. Edith didn't like the pigpen smell.

She wandered on, stopping to pick up a stick to tap against the pigpen fence.

The barn door was open. Inside it looked dark and cool. A hen pecked through the straw scattered on the floor. Edith put down her stick and knelt, calling to the hen as she had heard Faith and Alena do. She held out her hand, cupped as though filled with grain. "Here biddy, biddy, chick, chick, chick." The hen cocked her head to one side and surveyed Edith with a knowing eye. Then she began to peck again at the straw. Edith crept after her into the barn, calling softly, "Here biddy, biddy, chick, chick, chick." The hen paid no attention.

Edith plumped down in the straw and pulled her knees up under her skirt. She hugged her knees and sighed. It *was* cool in the barn, and she liked its dusty cow and horse smell. The stalls were empty. The stock was out to pasture, so there was nothing to be afraid of here. And no one to disturb, Edith thought. Not Vernon's grandma, not Vernon's puppy, not Vernon—not anyone to say, "Go away. Don't bother me. Leave *my* dog be."

The hen pecked her way out of sight. Edith sat, listening to the quiet emptiness of the barn and resting herself in its silence.

She was wondering if Vernon was still on the porch when she heard the sound. It was so faint she was not sure at first she truly heard something. She listened hard. Yes, there *was* a rustling, just the merest hint of a scratching somewhere near her feet. She flopped over, kneeling on elbows and knees, and put her ear to the barn floor. Just under her ear, she could hear quite clearly something rustling beneath the floor. She brushed the straw away. One plank had splintered, revealing a wide crack between the boards. She put her fingers in the crack and pried at the end of the plank. The wood was old and soft. It pulled up easily, and Edith heard a new sound— faint mewing cries. She leaned over to look into the hole she had made in the floor.

There, tucked beneath the planks, was a small, untidy pile of straw and fluffs of wool, paper torn in bits, and string, a piece of blue yarn, and some wisps of chicken down. Snuggled into the middle of the pile, squirming blindly over one another, was a litter of baby mice. Edith drew her breath in sharply. She scooted on hands and knees to the other side of the hole in the floor so that light from the open barn door would fall on the nest. She scrunched close to the hole and, wide-eyed, peered at the baby mice.

They were minute and pink and perfect—tiny perfect faces with sealed-shut eyes and sharp little noses and delicate ears, tiny little legs and wriggly little bodies and long naked pink tails. Tentatively, she poked them apart with her finger. Very, very gently, she touched each small warm body and counted them—one, two, three, four, five. Five baby mice.

"Oh," breathed Edith. "Oh."

Suddenly she wanted to show someone her discovery. She wanted to show Vernon. I found them, she thought, so they are mine. *My* baby mice. A puppy might be better than a doll, but what was a puppy to *five* baby mice?

Edith reached into the hole in the floor. She slid her fingers gently under the raggedy nest. Moving slowly and carefully, she scooped it up, cradling it in both hands. Then she stood up and walked out of the barn into the hot sunlight. She felt her way with her feet, her eyes fixed on her treasure. Her heart was thumping. My baby mice, she thought proudly. My very own baby mice.

Edith glanced toward the house. The porch was empty. But she saw John coming across the yard toward the barn. In her excitement, she called out to him, forgetting he frightened her with his stern, loud voice and frowning eyes.

"John! Brother John," she called. "See what I

found!" Edith held the nest up to John. "Only look," she said, breathless. "There's five of 'em. I found 'em in the barn. Aren't they dear?"

She gazed, delighted, at the nest in her hands. John's shadow fell across her. She looked up and saw his eyes widen, saw his brows draw together. She saw his large, white hand rise in the air and watched it sweep down in a great, curved arc. She cringed as the nest was dashed from her hands, and she watched his booted foot lift and descend on the tangle of straw and paper and tiny pink bodies.

John ground his foot on the nest. "Vermin!" he cried. "Filthy vermin!"

Edith stared at the flattened, unrecognizable heap of straw. Beads of sweat broke on her forehead and upper lip. The cold fingers of her extended hands stiffened. A cry strangled in her throat. "Mine!" She shook.

John was looking down at her. "Don't take on so," he was saying. "We cannot suffer vermin to live."

Edith's eyes were riveted to the nest. Her teeth chattered.

"Edith!" John said sharply. "That is enough! Edith!"

He shook her by the shoulders, and the blackness engulfed her.

5

Fits

EDITH came to consciousness in a room full of darkness and screaming. For a moment, she did not know where she was. She thought the screaming was part of the pain in her head. Then the baby hiccuped and quieted for a moment, and Edith knew, when the screaming began again, that the screaming was the baby and that this was the daybed in John-and-Alena's house and that the pain was something else.

She was lying on top of the quilt, and she was wearing her frock. Wearing her frock in bed! Someone had taken off her shoes, but she could feel her cotton stockings twisted about her legs. The curtains were drawn over the window, shutting out the afternoon sunlight but not its stuffy heat.

"Edie."

Someone was whispering her name.

"Edie, are you awake?"

Edith didn't answer. She turned her head and saw the comforting shape of Pansy Violet Rosebud on the pillow beside her. She reached for her doll and cuddled her, trying to think why she was here on her bed in the middle of the afternoon, still dressed, and why Alena didn't come to hush the baby. But her thoughts moved sluggishly. She had been playing in the barn. . . .

"Edie!" Vernon was standing beside the daybed.

"You shouldn't ought to be here," Edith said, her tongue slow and heavy in her mouth. That had been the first of John's many rules, laid down the first evening Edith lived in this house. Vernon must never go into the room assigned to Edith and the baby. And Edith must never go upstairs, where Vernon had his bed. "Your father catches you," Edith said, "you'll get a lickin' sure."

"Edie, you all right?"

Vernon seemed excited about something. Edith tried to think why he was acting so friendly.

"Head hurts," she said. "How come I'm in bed in my clothes?"

"Lordy, Lordy," Vernon whispered. He leaned close, so she could hear him over the baby's crying.

Edith knew John wouldn't like Vernon taking the Lord's name in vain, but she didn't say anything. All the rules seemed broken now.

Vernon was looking at Edith, up and down. "You had a fit," he said. "I saw you when Papa carried you into the house. You was a-twitchin' to beat the band, and your eyes looked funny." He peered into Edith's eyes, his own round with amazement. "Why'd ya do that, Edie?"

Edith sat up slowly, shaking her aching head. She held tightly to Pansy Violet Rosebud and wondered what a fit was and what Vernon meant when he said *she* had had one, but she felt afraid to ask. "I dunno," she said.

"Well," Vernon said, "it surely was somethin'

to see." His voice faltered. "Wish Baby'd stop cryin'. Mama's cryin' too, and Papa was yellin' at her, and Gran'ma has gone to her room. Gran'pa has gone for the doctor, but Papa said he oughtn't, and Mama said he ought, and no one's actin' right. Papa said a body'd think it was the M'llennium, the way Mama was carryin' on. He told me to get out from under foot. What's the M'llennium, Edie?"

They heard a door open and the sound of footsteps on bare floorboards. The baby hiccuped and quieted again. They heard Alena's voice.

Vernon looked about wildly, and suddenly Edith's head was clear. "The window," she said, and in a minute, Vernon had disappeared, only the swaying curtain showing where he had ducked beneath it on his way.

The door opened. It was Alena, and behind her was the doctor, the doctor who had come when Mother was sick. Edith's heart began to pound.

"Edie-love," Alena said. "Little Sister?"

At her call, Edith burst into tears. She dropped her doll and flung her arms around Alena's neck when Alena bent over the bed. She clung.

The baby began to scream again.

"I'm not sick," Edith cried. "Make him go away. I'm not sick."

"Of course you're not sick," the doctor said,

"but your sister says you've had a bad spell, and it won't hurt to reassure her."

Edith snuffled, holding tight to Alena.

"Why don't you take care of your baby, Mrs. Malcolm?" the doctor said.

Alena gave Edith a squeeze and loosened her arms. "He won't hurt you, Edie," she said. "He's here to help." She got up from the bed and went to tend the baby.

The doctor sat down where Alena had been, on the edge of the daybed. He picked Pansy Violet Rosebud off the floor where she had fallen and replaced her in Edith's arms. Putting his big hand on Pansy's cloth forehead, he looked thoughtful. "Her fall doesn't seem to have harmed her," he said, and then he put his hand on Edith's forehead. The hand felt all right to Edith, big and dry and cool. Edith watched Alena while the doctor examined her. Alena had picked up the baby and put her against her shoulder, patting her back and making soothing sounds. The baby subsided, hiccuping, resting her little head in the curve of Alena's neck. Edith could hear the baby's shuddering breaths in the silence of the hot, dim room.

The doctor put his ear to Edith's chest and listened. He tapped her back and chest. He looked down her throat and up her nose and into her eyes

and ears. Edith liked the sure, quick way his big
hands moved and the way he talked to her as he
worked. He listened attentively when she told him
again, "I'm not sick. Only my head hurts a little."
She no longer felt afraid.

"No, indeed," he agreed with her. "You aren't
sick." He turned to Alena, who stood anxiously by,
the baby on her shoulder. "The lungs are sound," he
said. "No sign of your mother's trouble."

"You'll be just fine," he said to Edith. "Try to
take a little nap, and I'll wager that headache will
go away. We'll get you something cool to drink."

He rose and nodded to Alena. "Mrs. Malcolm,
may I have a word with you?"

Edith could tell by the way they looked at one
another that the doctor was going to talk to Alena
about her. She remembered what Chester had said:
"We got a right to know. It's *us* they're decidin'
about." So even though she knew she wasn't supposed to, she slipped off the bed the moment they
had gone out, closing the door behind them. She
tiptoed to the door and put her ear to it.

"What it sounds like is fits," the doctor was
telling Alena in the hall. "Nothing to be done if it
is. A matter of a weak constitution. Feed her up.
Make her rest. You're a good nurse. You know what
to do."

"But . . ." Alena said. "But . . . fits? No one in our family has ever had fits. She's not feebleminded, Doctor. She's always been a right pert child." Edith could hear the worry in every word Alena spoke. It made her heart begin to thump again.

I'm not sick, she thought. I'm not sick.

"Perhaps it was the heat," the doctor said. "Perhaps it won't happen again."

But Edith's heart was thumping so loudly, she couldn't hear him. She crept back to the daybed and crawled again on top of the covers. She hugged Pansy Violet Rosebud. Holding the doll tight to her chest, she turned over and stared at the ceiling. She could feel her frock, clammy wet with sweat, hiked up under her armpits. *Thump, thump, thump,* her heart jumped in her chest, and with every beat she heard that scary-sounding word. Fits. Fits. Fits.

6

Supper

VERNON's Grandma Malcolm smelled bad.

Sitting next to her at the supper table, head bowed, hands folded, while John said interminable grace, Edith breathed through her mouth to avoid the smell. But the smell was a taste on the back of her tongue, and breathing through her mouth made Edith feel faint.

"In Christ Jesus' name, we pray. Amen," said John.

Grandma Malcolm stirred and raised her head, and her movements wafted the overpowering smell more strongly past Edith's nose.

Edith looked longingly across the table at the place beside Alena where Vernon sat. Vernon was watching John slice a thick slab of ham for the plate Alena held out to him. Alena spooned boiled potatoes and applesauce onto the plate and passed it to Vernon, who passed it to Grandpa Malcolm, who passed it to Edith. Edith took the warm heavy plate carefully in her hands and turned to give it to Grandma Malcolm. The rich meaty smell of the ham mingled with the smell of Grandma Malcolm and made Edith's stomach turn.

Grandma Malcolm's hands were tiny and wrinkled, grasping the plate Edith handed her. Edith thought Grandma Malcolm's hands and her small narrow feet did not seem to belong to the rest of her, which was huge and shapeless inside her dark heavy dress. Edith had to be careful not to knock over Grandma Malcolm's canes, which leaned against the table between them, as she passed the plate.

Grandpa Malcolm was holding out Edith's own plate. "Here you are, Edith," he said in his warm hearty voice. "Will you have some sour pickles or some butter and bread?"

Edith looked at her plate. The big pink slice of ham glistened with fat. Beside it, the rosy-colored applesauce swam into the steamy potatoes. Edith swallowed hard, fighting down the sickness that rose in her throat. She shook her head. She could not lift her hands to take the plate, but Grandpa Malcolm did not seem to notice. He set the plate before her, between her fork and her spoon, and turned to take his own plate from Vernon. He reached for the bowls of pickles and the basket of bread. He set about heaping his plate with sour pickles and green tomato preserves. He buttered a slice of bread and dribbled honey over it. He ladled gravy over ham and potatoes and began to eat. The food disappeared into his mouth in what seemed to Edith prodigious amounts. Chewing noisily, he smiled at Edith, who watched him, wide-eyed. "Eat up," he said around a mouthful of food.

Edith picked up her fork. She poked at a piece of potato and felt her stomach turn.

"Don't you feel well, Edie?" Alena said.

"Leave the child be!" said Grandma Malcolm, and Edith started at the sound of her querulous voice. "You make too much of her," said Grandma Malcolm. "Let her go without supper once or twice, and see if she eats. Alena, your mother spoiled the child, and you are taking up where she left off."

"Now, Missus . . ." protested Grandpa Malcolm.

But John spoke suddenly from the end of the table. "I quite agree with Mother," John said. "Far too much attention is paid to Edith."

Edith felt her face grow hot. She tried to lift her fork with its burden of cooling potato, but her hand was trembling, and the potato spilled onto the clean tablecloth.

Beside her, Grandma Malcolm made a small disgusted sound.

Vernon was chewing steadily, a satisfied look on his face.

"If you are not hungry, Edith," John said, "you may be excused from the table."

Edith put her fork down. The look on Alena's face told her that somehow she had made Alena unhappy. She lowered her eyes and concentrated on getting off of her chair without disturbing the dictionary.

"What do you say, Edith?" Grandma Malcolm demanded.

Edith lurched against the canes, sending them clattering to the floor in the silence that followed Grandma Malcolm's demand.

"Excuse me," whispered Edith. "Excuse me."

PANSY VIOLET ROSEBUD smiled at Edith from the daybed. Edith tiptoed into the room so as not to wake the baby, asleep in her crib. She climbed onto the daybed and took her doll in her arms.

Almost immediately, away from the sight and smell of food, Edith's stomach began to behave differently. The nausea was replaced by emptiness, peckish and cramped. Tears came to Edith's eyes. She wanted her supper. She wanted to go home. At home she had a big appetite. At home no one smelled bad.

From the dining room she could hear the clinking of dishes and cutlery. She could hear John's loud voice. She could hear Alena's murmur answering him. She sniffed the air, and she thought she could smell the spicy smell of ham and applesauce. And now they smelled delicious. *Now* they smelled good.

Rubbing her wet cheek against her doll's bonnet, she snuffled and sighed. "Poor Pansy Violet," she said. "You want your supper, don't you? Well, of course you do, you poor little thing."

Edith propped her doll against the pillow. She arranged the pink skirts of the doll's dress. "You sit right there while Mother fixes you a little bite,"

Edith told her. She began to set an imaginary table in front of her doll on a checkered blue square of the quilt. She poured an imaginary mug of milk and began to butter an imaginary slice of bread.

The door opened quietly, and Edith looked up to see Grandpa Malcolm's rosy face peering through the opening. Grandpa Malcolm's finger was on his lips. He looked behind himself hastily, then slipped into the room, moving quickly and lightly for so old and big a person, Edith thought. He came to the day-bed and put his hand out, resting it for a moment on the top of her head. Ordinarily, Edith did not like grown people to pat her head, but this was different—this brief warm touch. She looked up into Grandpa Malcolm's smiling eyes.

"Later," Grandpa Malcolm whispered, "you might get a wee bit hungry." He reached into his pocket and pulled something from it, something wrapped in his big clean handkerchief. He put it in her lap and put his finger to his lips again. Then, to Edith's astonishment, he winked.

She looked down at the handkerchief-wrapped object in her lap and touched it gingerly. When she looked up again, Grandpa Malcolm was gone, and the door to the hall was closing softly. Edith looked at the closed door for several moments, her head cocked to one side. "Well, I never . . ." she said to

Pansy Violet Rosebud, the way Mother used to say it to her when something surprising happened.

The baby was stirring, whimpering and turning her head from side to side. Edith glanced at her through the bars of the crib, then she unwrapped the handkerchief. It held a slice of ham between pieces of buttered bread. The ham was still warm. She could feel its moist warmth through the soft bread as she bit into it. The ham and buttery bread filled her mouth with goodness as she chewed and swallowed and bit and chewed and swallowed again. Her stomach began to feel warm and full.

The baby was starting to cry. She kicked out her legs and gathered a great, red-faced lungful of air and yelled.

Edith watched her, interested. "Shush, Baby," she said. "Are you hungry too?"

The baby hiccuped and seemed for a moment to be listening to Edith. Then she took another deep breath and yelled again.

"I'm coming. I'm coming," Edith heard Alena call, and then she heard the rapid tap of Alena's shoes on the floorboards of the hall.

Hastily Edith tucked the remnants of the sandwich and Grandpa Malcolm's handkerchief under the pillow. She whirled guiltily as the door sprang open and Alena hurried in.

But Alena did not go straight to the crib. She closed the door behind her and drew something from beneath her apron. "See if you can eat this, Edie-love," she said, putting a little bowl and a spoon on the table by the daybed. She bent and gave Edith a hug and a kiss. "It's rice pudding," she said, "the way you like it, with raisins and lots of cinnamon."

Edith felt a little lump in her throat. Alena wasn't unhappy with her after all. "Thank you," she said, and Alena smiled and put her finger to her lips.

Alena picked up the baby. "Goodness," she said, "she's positively swimming—wet clear through! Edie, get me a dry diaper and slip, will you, love. No wonder you're making such a big fuss, little one."

Edith hopped down from the daybed and began to help Alena change the baby.

The rice pudding was wonderful! Edith sat on the daybed and ate it, pretending to give Pansy Violet Rosebud a spoonful now and then, when Alena had taken the baby away to her room to nurse. Edith scraped the spoon carefully around the bowl, gathering every last sweet transparent grain of rice.

"Hey!" whispered someone at the window. "Hey, Edie, you in there? Hey!"

Edith crawled to the foot of the daybed and lifted a corner of the curtain at the open window. The light outside was failing, and a moth blundered in toward the lamp Alena had lighted on the table.

"Hey!" said Vernon from outside the window. "Want this?" He tossed something through the window, and it landed near Edith's knee. Edith looked down at an apple, round and shiny and red.

Edith picked up the apple. It felt cool in her hand. She leaned forward and poked her head through the window. She saw Vernon disappear around the corner of the house. "Vernon," she called after him. "Hey, Vernon!"

But the yard was empty except for a hen fluttering to roost in the branches of the oak.

Edith looked again at the apple in her hand. "Vernon?" she whispered, her forehead wrinkling in puzzlement.

The lamplight flickered on the empty bowl and spoon. It picked out the white folds of Grandpa Malcolm's handkerchief. It made a golden glow on the smooth skin of the apple in Edith's hand.

"Well, I never . . ." Edith said to Pansy Violet Rosebud, and—although it might have been a trick of lamplight and shadow—Edith thought she saw the doll wink.

7

A Story

"TELL US A STORY, 'Lena. Tell us, do,"
begged Edith.

The kitchen was yellow with lamplight, and
the windows were lightly steamed. It was Saturday
night, bath night, and Grandma and Grandpa Malcolm were dozing in the sitting room. John had gone
to town. Alena was bending over the kitchen table
bathing the baby. Edith, in her nightdress with her

hair loose and brushed shining for the night, stood beside her and held the towel.

"Perhaps," said Alena, lifting the baby from the pan of water. The lamplight reflected from the baby's rosy-wet skin. She chuckled and kicked her legs. Edith held up the towel to wrap the baby in.

A blanket hung on a low line strung between the coat hooks by the door and the stovepipe. Vernon's face appeared over the top of the blanket. His hair was slickered wet to his head, and there was soap in his ears. "Papa says not to tell stories," he said.

Edith held her breath, waiting to see what Alena would say.

Alena looked at Vernon. Her voice was very thoughtful. "Your father is mistaken about stories, Son," she said. "A story is not a lie, but make-believe. There is a difference."

Edith let her breath out deeply. Of course there's a difference, she thought. She looked at Vernon's bath-wet, doubtful face. "Don't you *like* stories?" she asked.

Alena was patting the baby's hair and face with the towel.

Edith took a corner of the towel and dried the baby's pink little feet.

"When I was a little girl, our mother used to tell us stories," Alena said.

Edith nodded. "Me too," she said, and her throat felt tight.

"John does not approve. . . ." Alena said. Her voice had gotten quiet, and Edith realized she was looking at Vernon. "If we have stories from time to time now Edie's come to live with us, your papa need not be concerned," she said to Vernon.

Vernon looked skeptical.

"The stories would be just for us," said Alena. She laid the kicking baby on the table. "Hand me a diaper, will you, Edie?" she said. "And you, young man, let's have a bit more scrubbing, if you please."

Vernon's head disappeared behind the blanket. Edith heard a splash as he plunked down in the tub of water.

The baby fretted, and Alena leaned over her, crooning and blowing gently into her face until she smiled.

"*May* we have a story, 'Lena?" Edith asked again.

Alena's voice was clear and decided. "Yes," she said. "Yes, I believe we will . . . as soon as everyone has had his bath."

"I had my bath already," Edith said, speaking

loudly so Vernon would hear. "I scrubbed myself."

Behind the blanket, the water sloshed. "*I'm* scrubbing," Vernon said. "I can scrub myself as good as Edie."

When the baby was dressed in her nightdress, Alena let Edith sit in the rocker beside the stove, with the baby in her arms. Alena carried a towel to Vernon and helped him dry himself and pull on his nightshirt.

Edith held her baby niece carefully. The baby was warm and sleepy. Her round, hard head felt heavy against Edith's shoulder. Edith rubbed her cheek against the baby's silky hair. The rocking chair, set in motion by a shove from Alena, was slowing, but Edith was afraid to arch against the chair-back to make it move. She must not drop the baby. She must be very good and very grown-up so she could continue to hold the baby in her arms.

And soon, Alena would tell them a story.

Alena was dumping the heavy tub of water off the side of the back porch. A cool breeze blew through the kitchen from the open back door, and Edith tucked the baby's shawl more tightly. Alena took down the blanket, folded it, and sent Vernon to put it away in the blanket chest. She wiped up the spilled water while Vernon padded about importantly, hanging wet towels on the line by the stove.

At last, Alena pulled up another chair. She called to Vernon to come sit on the rug at her feet.

The warmth of the stove had reddened Edith's cheeks and made her eyelids heavy. She opened her eyes wide and licked her lips and gazed at Alena.

"Once, long ago and far away . . ." Alena began.

Edith sighed when she heard the familiar words. She snuggled the baby close.

". . . a pretty young girl named Cinderella lived with her wicked stepmother and two very ugly stepsisters . . ." Alena said, and she told how badly Cinderella's sisters treated her and how Cinderella wept in the ashes of the hearth and was left home from the ball.

Vernon scooted close and laid his head against his mother's knee and listened.

Edith closed her eyes. She let herself feel sad for Cinderella. She imagined the rags and the terrible hard work and the disappointment of being left home. She felt very sorry for Cinderella. She waited with held breath for the fairy godmother to come. When at last Alena was telling them how beautiful the fairy was and how she waved her magic wand to turn Cinderella's rags to a lovely ball gown, Edith shivered with delight. She imagined the gown was pink, *her* most favorite color.

"When the pumpkin coach was standing before them, all golden and shining in the moonlight," Alena said, "her fairy godmother asked Cinderella to go into the pantry and find six little mice. . . ."

Edith's heart stopped. "Mice?" she whispered, clutching the baby. She had forgotten *this* part.

Alena smiled. "Yes," she said. "Dear little mice with little pink noses and long pink tails. She wanted them for the horses, you see. . . . Edie, what's the matter?"

Edith shook her head. "For the horses?"

"Yes, for the horses. The fairy godmother waved her wand and said some magic words and there, right in front of Cinderella's eyes, those six little mice were changed to horses. Six beautiful white horses to pull the pumpkin coach!"

"Horses," said Edith, wonderingly. "She waved her wand, and they changed to horses. . . ."

Alena nodded. "Yes, and then she sent Cinderella to find two big fat rats to turn into footmen for the coach. . . ."

Alena's voice went on, but Edith was remembering the scratchy feeling of a straw and string nest in her hands. She remembered a big white hand— or was it a wand?—waving toward her. She remembered the emptiness where a moment before her hands had been full. Alena's voice filled her head, lilting with the rhythm of the story. Turned them into horses for the pumpkin coach, Edith thought.

"And so," said Alena, "Cinderella and her prince lived happily ever after."

8
Laying Up Treasures

EDITH woke early to a breeze that ruffled the limp white curtains at the open window. She felt it whisper like a delicious secret across her bare legs. The coolness and the fresh smell of the breeze breathed deep into her chest, and suddenly her eyes flew open with the realization of what day it was. She sat up and swung her legs over the edge of the daybed.

Faithie's coming! she wanted to shout to the baby. It's threshing day, and Faithie's coming to help cook for the crew!

But the baby was curled in a plump, rosy tangle of round limbs and bedclothes, her face blank and slack-mouthed with sleep. The baby did not care.

"*I'm* glad Faithie's coming!" Edith whispered to herself. She twirled on the cool floor in her bare feet and hugged herself tight.

It did not take long to wash in the china basin on the commode. Edith pulled on her drawers and chemise and petticoats. She felt for her dress, laid ready on the chair, and shrugged it over her head. Unbuttoned, she carried her shoes and stockings with her as she tiptoed to the door.

Alena was already in the kitchen. Sunlight was just beginning to stream through the windows. It touched the row of naked, headless chickens cooling on the kitchen table. It lit the columns of steam that rose from the pots, bubbling on the stove. Alena was adding kindling to the fire. She straightened and wiped her hands on her apron.

" 'Morning, Edie," she said. "Need buttoning?"

Edith glanced around the kitchen. "Is this the day, 'Lena? Is this the day Faithie comes?"

"This is the day, Edie-love. This is the day Faith comes . . . *and* the threshing crew!"

Edith sighed happily. "I'm hungry," she said.

"Me too," said Vernon from the doorway. "I'm *starved!*"

Edith was sitting on the floor after breakfast, struggling with her shoe buttons, when she heard a buggy in the yard. Before she could hook the last button, Faith was at the kitchen door, a basket over her arm. Edith dropped the buttonhook with a clatter and ran to hug her around the waist.

"Edie, Edie, let her get through the door," Alena chided, laughing, and came to take the heavy basket from their sister's arm.

"What on earth have you got here?" Alena exclaimed as she lugged the heavy basket to the table and thumped it down next to the chickens. Edith saw Vernon come shyly forward and climb on a chair to peer into the basket.

"Oh, just a few things," Faith said. "I thought an extra pie or so wouldn't hurt, and the greengages are ripe." Faith lifted the cloth that covered the basket and set out the pies, three of them, their warmth attesting that she had been up before dawn to bake. The greengage plums, plump and golden, filled a string bag. She handed one each to Edith and Vernon and Alena. Then she polished another on her skirt for herself.

Edith sank her teeth into the sweetness of the

plum and tasted home. The juice ran down her chin.

Faith was still pulling things from the basket. "I hope Edith hasn't grown out of these," she said, holding up a small stack of pinafores and stockings. "They were in the mending. No doubt all she brought with her are in *your* mending by now. And, oh, yes. . . . Here, Edie, I thought you'd want this."

Edith's heart thumped with happiness as Faith lifted her knitted afghan out of the basket. Edith held out her arms and buried her face in it. The soft rose-colored wool felt warm against Edith's cheek. It smelled like home.

"And these," Faith said. Her spectacles caught the sunlight with a happy glitter as she piled the old one-armed baby on top of the afghan, and Edith's ball and box of dominos.

"My things!" Edith said.

Faith took one more object from her basket. It was a basket, too, though much, much smaller— Mother's Chinese basket in which she had kept her thimbles and needles and threads. "Mother would have wanted you to have these, Edie," she said, placing the basket on the edge of the table where Edith could see into it. She lifted off its lid. Inside the basket were more of Mother's things.

Edith put her afghan and toys on a chair and came to stand by the table. She put out her hand and stroked the cool, blue-beaded tassels of the Chinese basket's lid.

"For you from Mother," Alena said, taking out of the basket and putting into her hand a small golden brooch. "Because you, like Mother, love pretty things."

Edith looked up at Alena and Faith and saw that they were smiling, with tears trembling in their eyes. She reached into the basket and pulled out a long blue ribbon. The ribbon was smooth and silky in her fingers. A piece of sky that will not fade, Edith thought.

There was a tiny New Testament in the Chinese basket. Edith put down the brooch and the ribbon and picked it up. Its gilt-edged pages were soft with use. Edith riffled them with her fingers. She remembered Mother reading silently from the little book sometimes of an evening. She remembered the fire lighting the edges of the pages with a golden glow. The beauty and the pain of it clutched in Edith's chest. Her heart was bursting, she thought, with sadness and happiness. She tried to say thank you. She tried to lift her head, to look at her sisters, to open her mouth, but the clutching cut off her breath, and her fingers and toes were tingling with cold. The blackness was weighing on her. The blackness and the cold . . .

They were bending over her when she opened her eyes. Alena was there and Faith and Vernon. Their faces were white and shocked.

"Are you all right?" Faith was saying urgently, and there were tears on Alena's cheeks.

"Lordy!" Vernon said. "Lordy!" and no one told him to shush.

Edith blinked, and pain forked behind her eyes like a lightning flash. She struggled to sit up, and Faith helped her. She rubbed a hurting place on her arm and saw a bruise spreading beneath her skin. Had someone hit her? Knocked her down? She glared at Vernon.

"Lordy, Edie, you done it again!" Vernon said. "You had a fit!"

"Did not," Edith muttered, her tongue unwieldy in her mouth. She reached for her afghan heaped on the chair and tried to get up.

Alena put out her hand, as though to help her.

Edith jerked away. "Did not," Edith said. "Did *not* have a fit!"

THE BUZZ of a fly vexed Edith awake. She lay still, eyes closed, and took stock. She was on the porch settee, where Alena and Faith had made her rest. The pain in her head had dulled. The noon sunlight glared red through her scratchy eyelids. She was sweaty and hot, and her mouth had a nasty taste.

There were voices beneath the buzz of the fly. With an effort, Edith raised her hand, which felt swollen and heavy, to brush the fly away. It seemed too much effort to open her eyes. She listened to the voices—Alena and Faith. Faith . . . Faith had come to visit, to help Alena with the cooking. . . . Faith had brought Edith's afghan. . . . Edith remembered. I must have fallen asleep, she thought. I must have fallen asleep on the settee.

Another voice sounded so near that Edith started. "Mind you fasten those cloths with pins," the voice commanded, "lest the wind blow them off." It was an old, unpleasant voice—unhappy, Edith thought. Grandma Malcolm's voice.

What wind? Edith wondered.

Edith heard her sisters again. They were calling to Grandma Malcolm, but their words were lost in the still noon heat.

Edith stirred and once more lifted her hand, this time to rub her eyes open. She heard the irritated creak of Grandma Malcolm's rocking chair and Grandma Malcolm's aggravated snort. She smelled Grandma Malcolm's nasty smell. Holding her head carefully so as not to jar loose its ache, Edith sat up and looked about her. Grandma Malcolm was sitting a few feet away, sewing. The baby napped in a basket beside her chair. Edith could see Alena and Faith spreading cloths on the plank and trestle tables ranged under the oak trees in the yard.

"Awake, are you?" Grandma Malcolm said. She shook her head, her wrinkled lips thin. "What *will* you think of next to avoid making yourself of some use?"

Edith caught her breath at the pain that flared behind her eyes. The blood rushed to her cheeks. "I didn't . . ." she started to say, but Grandma Malcolm's face was hard and closed. She did not look at Edith, and her tiny feet pushed furiously against the porch, making her chair rock.

Edith bowed her head to hide her threatening tears. Through their shimmer she saw the Chinese basket Faith had put on the end of the settee, "where you can see it when you wake up," Faith had said. Edith pulled the basket toward her. Mine, she thought, comforting herself. This is mine. She rocked her body to ease herself.

She could hear the voices of her sisters, low and worried, coming toward her across the yard. She lifted her head and saw them, walking arm in arm, their heads bent together, talking earnestly. She guessed they were talking about her. The pain behind her eyes throbbed as she tried to make out what they said, tried to read the words on their lips. She could tell from the slow, sad way they walked that the day was spoiled. The wonderful visit with Faithie was spoiled, and she, Edith, had spoiled it.

"You had a fit," Vernon had said before Alena shushed him. Edith ducked her head, her face burning with shame, and lifted the lid from the Chinese basket. Edith took out the little Testament. A book of my own, she thought. She wished she could read from it, as Mother used to. The book fell open in her hands, and Edith saw a pansy someone—Mother, perhaps—had saved and pressed between the pages.

" 'Lay not up for yourselves treasures upon earth,' " said Grandma Malcolm suddenly, and Edith felt her small, pale eyes sharp upon her.

The Testament fell, open, into Edith's lap.

Edith knew what Grandma Malcolm was saying. Grandma Malcolm and John often quoted words from the Bible. They were God's words Grandma Malcolm was saying, God's words from the Bible. "Lay not up for yourselves treasures. . . ."

These were Mother's *treasures*—this book, this basket, these pretty things. And look what had happened to Mother. Edith thought of what had been happening to her . . . since she found the mice, the mice she had wanted for her own. Since Faith had

brought her her things, her own treasures. Treasures.

Treasures and fits. "Lordy!" Vernon had said.
"You had a fit!" Edith knew a fit was an ugly,
shameful thing to have. She knew it from the way
they looked at her, from the way Vernon was
shushed when he said the word, from Alena's voice
telling the doctor, "No one in *our* family has ever
had fits."

"Lay not up for yourselves treasures. . . ." The
words rang threateningly in Edith's head as she
closed the Testament on the dried little face of the
pansy. The sunlight picked out the gilt lettering on
the Testament cover. She put it into the basket. Edith
set her mouth. She put the lid on the basket. Then
she leaned over the edge of the settee and put the
basket on the floor.

Alena and Faith were coming up the steps. See-
ing her awake, they frowned. "How are you feeling,
Edie-love?" Alena said, and Edith heard Grandma
Malcolm mutter.

"I'm all better now," Edith said. "May I get
up?"

If Alena said she might get up, she would put
the basket away, she thought. She would put the
basket, and her afghan and toys and . . . and Pansy

Violet Rosebud, too . . . away where she couldn't play with them. She would not lay up treasures ever again, she thought. And Grandma Malcolm and John would be pleased with her. And God would be pleased. And there would be no more fits.

9

Contention

ALENA's needle stabbed into the flannel of John's shirt in tiny vicious bites. Edith watched the needle, fascinated, her own work idle in her hands.

Clearly Alena was vexed about something. She had been silent all during supper, but her fork had rung against her plate, and as she washed up after supper the dishes had clashed together dangerously and the soapy water in the enamel dishpan had sloshed and foamed.

Edith glanced at the others, searching for a clue to what was wrong with Alena. Grandma and Grandpa Malcolm rocked in chairs drawn up to the grate. There was a nip in the air mornings and evenings now—"The chill gets in my bones," complained Grandma Malcolm—so just that day Grandpa Malcolm had brought the heating stove out of the shed, where it had been stored for the summer, and had set it up in the sitting room while Grandma Malcolm fussed about the soot he got on the carpet.

It was not the soot that had upset Alena. "A fire will feel good," Alena had said.

Vernon was sprawled on the carpet at Grandpa Malcolm's feet, playing at cat's cradle with a piece of string. Vernon had not been naughty all day. He had even let Edith play with the puppy. Alena was not cross with him.

John sat at the table in the yellow lamplight. He was frowning over the figures he made on a piece of paper with a pencil he had whittled to a fine sharp point, but John often frowned when he worked at his figures and books. Edith did not *think* it was John who had made Alena angry. Still, it was John's shirt that Alena's needle so fiercely stabbed.

"I have hired Harold Streeter to help with the corn, Father," John said, his voice so loud and sudden that Edith jumped. She flushed and fixed her eyes on the salt sack she was hemming for a handkerchief, hoping John had not noticed. But John was not looking at her. He was looking at Grandpa Malcolm, who had ceased rocking and was leaning forward in his chair, rubbing his hands before the fire.

"We can't afford a dollar a day for hired labor, John," Grandpa Malcolm said. "Not when you get only a dollar and a quarter at the school."

"It's a dollar and a quarter a day for nine months," John said. "We'll only need Harold for a week or so. School commences next week, and I am not going to shirk the teaching, Father. You can't get the corn in by yourself."

Grandpa Malcolm turned his hands in the firelight and examined the palms. He did not look at John as he spoke. "If'n we worked Sundays as well as Saturdays . . ."

"And I am not going to desecrate the Sabbath, Father."

Edith, watching from under her lashes, saw Grandma Malcolm nod approvingly.

"Gol durn it, John," Grandpa Malcolm said, and now he was looking at John. "Seems to me if the good Lord sends a harvest like this'n, he can't mind if we work a couple of Sundays to get it in. If'n you're bound to school-teach at the busiest time of the year, leastways we could use the days we have to advantage."

Now it was John who did not look at Grandpa Malcolm. " 'And God blessed the seventh day, and sanctified it: because that in it he had rested from all his work,' " he quoted, and Grandma Malcolm said, "Amen."

Grandpa Malcolm sighed and leaned back in his chair. "Then I wish't He'd take a rest from the ripenin' of the corn," he muttered. "It seems to grow Sundays, same as any other day."

The clock ticked loudly in the silence that followed. Edith concentrated on making her stitches small and neat and making herself as small and quiet as she could be. She tried to make even her breathing small.

All the grown-ups looked angry now, except for Grandma Malcolm, who had a small tight smile on her lips and a bland, satisfied look on her face. Presently she began to rock, and the rocking made a steady creaking sound in rhythm with the clock. John's pencil scratched.

Edith was thinking of school. Her breath had caught in her throat when Grandpa Malcolm mentioned it. John was a schoolmaster, Edith knew. He taught at the Brown School, where Vernon had told her he went last year. "It's the nuts," Vernon had said, "havin' your own father for a teacher. I wish't I could go to the Elvaston School like you."

Edith had not told him she did not go to the Elvaston School—that she had never, in fact, been to school at all. "Next year," Faith had said. "You can go next year when Mother is well."

Edith smoothed her stitches with her fingers. They *would* go crooked and big, in spite of all her care. She wondered if she was to go to school this year. Mother had not gotten well. . . .

Edith looked longingly at the shelf of books beneath the window. If she could read, she would not have to wait until Alena had time to tell stories. She could have a story whenever she wished if she could read. Still, going to school to John would be scary, she thought. The nuts, like Vernon said.

John was putting away his papers and pencil. He was opening the big Bible before him on the table. "It is time for devotions," he said.

Alena's needle flashed in and out of the cloth of John's shirt. Grandma Malcolm was folding her work and putting it away, and Grandpa Malcolm was shifting in his chair as though trying to get comfortable. Vernon sat up and scooted close to Alena's knee, stuffing his string into his pocket. Edith did not know whether to put away her salt-sack handkerchief or not. In confusion, she waited to see what Alena would do. Alena smoothed a seam with tense white fingers as John began to read.

" 'Wives, submit yourselves unto your own husbands, as unto the Lord,' " John read.

Edith heard the sharp expulsion of Alena's breath. Alena began to pack her threads and thimble into her workbasket, her fingers moving jerkily. Edith folded her own piece of work, sticking the needle through the folds, and took off her own thimble. She handed them to Alena and saw how Alena's hands shook as she took them. Alena's face was set, and a blue vein throbbed beneath the skin of her temple.

" 'Nevertheless,' " read John, " 'let every one of you in particular so love his wife even as himself; *and the wife see that she reverence her husband.*' " John's voice rose loud and emphatic as he read these last words. He closed the Bible firmly.

"Amen," said Grandma Malcolm. "Amen."

"Father," said John, "will you lead us in prayer?"

Grandpa Malcolm jerked. Edith saw he had dozed off during the reading. "Of course, of course!" he said, rather more heartily than called for, and he creaked stiffly to his knees.

Grandma Malcolm bowed her head and folded

her tiny hands. Alena rose and knelt, and Vernon scrambled to kneel beside her. John pushed his chair away from the table and knelt beside it, propping his elbows on the chair and resting his head in his hands.

Edith slipped off her stool. She wanted to kneel close to Alena, but she could feel the anger like waves from Alena's taut body. She knelt by her stool.

"Our Heavenly Father," Grandpa Malcolm intoned.

What *was* the matter with Alena? Edith peeped from beneath her lowered lids as Grandpa Malcolm prayed. She could not see Alena's face now, only the clenched fingers of her clasped hands. Edith listened carefully for the end of the prayer, and when it came she was ready.

"In Christ Jesus' name we pray," Grandpa Malcolm said, and Edith's voice piped in with the rest to say, "Amen."

10

School

THROUGH the bedroom wall, Edith could hear their voices. Alena's was angry and choked with tears. John's was calm and firm and loud.

"But she's ill, John," Alena said. "Something is terribly wrong with her. What if she had a . . . a fainting spell at school!"

Edith pulled Alena's blue quilt over her ears.

So that was what Alena was vexed about: John was going to make Edith go to school. Edith burrowed her head into the pillow and tried not to listen, but she couldn't help it. Their voices were too loud.

"What if she *does* have a fit at school?" John said reasonably. "She seems unharmed by them, so long as she doesn't hurt herself falling. She is not ill, Alena."

"She is," Alena cried. "She must be. Why else does she have these . . . spells?"

I'm not sick, Edith thought. I'm not.

"Edith is not ill, and she is not feebleminded," John was saying. "I have observed the child. She is perfectly intelligent. It is past time she went to school. Indeed, I cannot understand what your family has been thinking of to keep her out so long. She shall go to school, Alena. So long as she lives under my roof, she *shall* go to school."

Edith could hear Alena crying. It was an angry, hopeless crying that made Edith's stomach feel sick.

"She'll have a fit one day at school," Alena cried, "and the other children will laugh and taunt her. They'll call her names and whisper about her behind her back and carry the tale home. It isn't right, John. She shouldn't be made to endure it. It isn't right!"

"It isn't right that a child of her age cannot read or write," John said. "Not a child of my family!"

"Then teach her at home," Alena cried. "I will do it. Let me teach her at home."

There was cold finality in John's voice. "Enough of this," he said. "Edith shall go to school next week with Vernon, and that's the end of it!"

Edith shivered. She felt like crying herself. I don't want the children to laugh at me, she thought. Alena says they will, and Alena must know. But I do want to go to school. Edith's mouth felt dry, and her stomach was sick.

She turned over. She could see the white iron bars of the baby's crib gleaming palely through the dark. She could hear the baby's stuffy breathing and the small, whimpery baby sounds she made in her sleep. The voices from John-and-Alena's room had stopped. Edith listened until she could hear a roaring in her ears, but she could not hear them now. She could not hear Alena crying. She could not hear the rustle of their bed's straw tick.

I put away my afghan and Mother's basket and my toys, Edith thought. I'm not laying up treasures any more, and if I don't have a fit, the children won't laugh. They won't even know. At school I could learn to read stories. I could take my lunch in a pail just like Vernon, and I could sit at a desk. She remembered all that Chester and Vernon had told her about going to school. There might be girls my age, she thought. And then the fear returned, like a shiver down her back. If I had a fit, they would laugh and stare. If I had a fit . . . Edith pushed the fear away. She pulled the quilt tight around her. I won't have a fit, she thought. Not ever again. And at school I could play with the girls at recess-time. We could play ring-a-ring o' roses. We could play dare-base and one-ole-cat.

Edith's shoulders and feet were getting warm beneath Alena's blue quilt. The small ticklish feeling in her stomach didn't feel so much like sickness now. Just as she sank into sleep, Edith remembered what John had called her. "A child of *my* family," he had said.

FROM the fields of timothy on either side of the road, the clatter of machinery and the voices of men rose out of clouds of dust. The fields were a gold and brown haze behind the fences Edith hurried past. The turbid air smelt cider-spicy with new-cut hay and apples and smoke. Ahead in the thicket behind the schoolhouse, the hard maples flamed against the gold of the elms.

"Don't dawdle, Vernon," said John, and Edith wondered how he knew without looking that Ver-

non had stopped at the corner of the split-rail fence
to pick a blackberry. John strode ahead of them on
the road. "Hurry along," he called over his shoulder
to Vernon.

Vernon popped the berry into his mouth, wiped
his hand on his brand-new trousers, and ran to catch
up.

Edith was almost running too, just to keep John
in sight. Her breath came in gasps, and her thin legs
pumped steadily beneath her newly lengthened
skirt. "She should have a new frock," Alena had
fretted, but there hadn't been time. Instead, Alena
had let down her last year's madras plaid. A row of
black braid covered the faded line where the old
hem had turned. Alena had tied Edith's hair with
the leftover braid. "My, you look nice," she had said
this morning when Edith was dressed. "You look
real nice for your first day of school." Alena's mouth
had smiled, and her voice had been bright, but Edith
thought her eyes looked funny—sad or scared, the
way Edith felt now, hurrying along behind John.

Vernon's shoes scuffed in the powdery dust.
"Nuts!" she heard him say under his breath. "Nuts.
Nuts. Nuts!"

John was already on the schoolhouse steps.
Edith saw him unlock the tall, narrow doors. She
saw him go inside.

Edith's heart skipped a beat, and suddenly her legs would not obey her. Her feet stumbled to a halt, and Vernon brushed past her, waving.

"Hey," he cried. "Hey there!"

There were children on the schoolhouse steps. Edith stood at the edge of the schoolyard and stared at them.

"Vernon," she tried to say. "Vernon, wait for me." But her voice was a whisper, and Vernon didn't wait.

The children were greeting him. A boy jumped up and punched his shoulder. The girls smiled and spoke. More boys and girls were approaching on the road, and two big boys astride a blaze-faced mare rode across the neighboring field, shouting. Their voices came to Edith in a babble. She saw two girls embracing. She saw three boys scuffling together on the steps.

Edith's frock felt hot and tight around her neck. No one else wore plaid, she saw. The frocks of the other girls were checked or sprigged or plain. *Their* frocks were all new, Edith was sure—new for the first day of school.

John appeared again at the top of the steep schoolhouse steps. The morning sun glinted gold on his hair and on the large round watch he held in one hand, marking the time. "Let us commence," John called in his loudest, firmest voice; and the children—even the biggest boys and girls—fell silent and began to file up the steps.

John looked out over their heads, squinting into the sun. Edith felt his eyes, clear and pale, rest on her. She saw one eyebrow lift.

His look set her legs in motion. Alone, Edith hurried across the schoolyard to the foot of the steps. When she looked up at the doorway, John had gone inside. The last big boy was going through the door. Edith scuttled up the steps and slipped inside behind him.

The cloakroom entryway was dark after the glare of the yard. Edith paused for a moment beside the door until she could see again. In the schoolroom, the children were jostling into their seats, two to a desk. Edith searched for Vernon, but she could not find him. All the desks were filled!

"There is an empty seat here, Edith," John said, his voice ringing out over the excited whispers of the children.

Edith thought they all looked at her. She blushed and stumbled toward the place in the front row that John was indicating. A girl was sitting on one side of the desk. Edith slipped awkwardly into the other side, keeping her eyes on the floor. The splintery edge of the seat snagged her stocking and scratched her leg. Mortified, Edith felt to see if her stocking was torn.

"Good morning, pupils," John said, and once again the power of his voice silenced the children. Edith heard it like a roar in her head, and her heart quaked. She glanced sideways at the girl beside her and saw the girl's hand move in her lap. The fingers of the hand fluttered in a tiny greeting. Lifting her eyes, Edith saw that the girl was looking at her from the corner of her eyes. The girl smiled.

"School is in session," John said. "We will commence with the calling of the roll."

11
An Accident

"CLASS DISMISSED," John said.

The room, which a moment before had been silent, stirred to life. A big boy hurried to the door and flung it open. As the first children pushed their way out into the sunlight, Edith heard a joyous whoop.

Edith's seatmate put her book and slate into her

satchel. " 'Bye, Edith," she said as she stood up. "See you tomorrow."

"Oh, yes," said Edith, her happiness like a bubble in her chest. "See you tomorrow, Rosa. Tomorrow."

Because tomorrow Edith could come to school again. And tomorrow and tomorrow and tomorrow, Edith thought. She watched Rosa join the throng of children at the door. Tomorrow she and Rosa would play at recess and eat their lunches with the other girls under the black-oak tree as they had done today. Tomorrow Edith would learn some more letters and practice them on her slate. She sighed and wiped her slate clean. Through the open windows she could hear the children shouting in the schoolyard. She could hear the laughter and the joshing of the boys.

"Joh . . . Mr. Malcolm," Edith said, raising her hand the way pupils must and remembering to call John "Mister." "May I take my slate home to practice my letters?"

John did not look up from his ledger. "Yes, Edith, you may," he said. "Run along home now with Vernon. I will follow shortly."

Edith put her slate pencil into the pocket of her pinafore and settled her slate in the crook of her arm the way she had seen the other girls do. She slipped out of her desk and looked for Vernon. He was not in his seat in the back row. Perhaps he was waiting outside.

Edith stood at the top of the steps and scanned the yard. Vernon was not with the boys who were saddling their mare over by the shed. He was not under the black-oak or in the neighboring field or walking up the road.

"Vernon," she called. "Where are you, Vernon? Wait for me."

Edith trailed down the steps. Had Vernon already started for home? Had he gone home without her?

"After school I shall have work to do. You and Edith must walk home together," John had told Vernon this morning. "You know the way, and Edith does not."

"Vernon!" Edith called, peering around the corner of the schoolhouse. Perhaps he had gone to the privy, she thought.

The privy was tucked discreetly among the trees in the thicket behind the schoolhouse. Edith followed the path beaten through the tall grass.

"Vernon," she called. "Vernon!"

"Go away," said Vernon's voice from inside the privy. There was something wrong. Vernon's voice sounded odd. "Go away," he said.

"Vernon Malcolm, you come out this instant," Edith said. "You're supposed to walk me home."

"Go away," said Vernon, and Edith knew what was wrong with his voice. He was crying. "Go away, pest!"

Edith looked back at the schoolhouse. John was nowhere in sight. "It's all right," she said softly. "Your papa can't see us." She knew girls and boys were not to go out to the privy together. It was one of John's rules, at school and at home.

Edith heard Vernon sniffling. "What's the matter, Vernon?" she said. "Did you hurt yourself?"

"Go home," Vernon cried. "Edie, go home!"

"I can't. I don't know the way!"

There was silence from the privy and then, again, sniffling. The privy door opened a crack.

Vernon's face, white and smudged with tears, appeared in the crack. "Just follow the road to the lane past Mr. Choate's barn," Vernon said. "It's easy, Edie. Please go home." Vernon's eyes were red.

Edith frowned. "You *are* hurt," she said. "Did you get in a fight?" Chester had gotten in a fight once at school. His lip had been split.

"I'm not hurt," Vernon said. "Please go home, Edie. Please go home."

"I'm going to tell your papa," Edith said. "You've been in a fight." She turned.

"No! No, Edie, please!" The privy door banged open, and Vernon came hurtling out. "Edie!"

Edith turned back and looked at Vernon. He wasn't bleeding, and his clothes weren't dirty or torn, only . . .

Vernon hung his head. His face turned a deep beet red. "I . . . I . . . had an accident," he said, so softly that Edith could scarcely hear him.

"Oh," Edith said, her eyes going to the wetness that stained his new trousers.

Vernon's shoulders began to shake, and Edith saw tears running down his cheeks and dripping from his nose and chin.

"Oh my!" Edith said.

"I forgot to go at recess," Vernon said, scrubbing fiercely at his eyes. "I jumped up as soon as school let out, but . . ."

Edith nodded. John did not allow the children to leave the classroom for any reason. It was another rule. She stepped forward and put her hand on Vernon's shoulder. "Don't cry, Vernon. I won't tell."

Vernon was feeling in his pockets for a handkerchief. Edith handed him hers. He blew his nose. "It don't matter," he said. "Papa'll find out anyways. Have the fellas all gone?"

Edith looked back at the schoolyard and the

road. The boys and their mare were gone. The road was empty.

"They've gone, I think," she said.

Vernon stuffed her handkerchief into his pocket. His shoulders slumped. "I'm gonna get such a lickin'," he said.

Edith looked at Vernon's forlorn face. "It wasn't your fault," she said. "Sometimes I can't wait either."

"Don't matter," Vernon said. "I'm gonna get a lickin' anyways."

Edith grabbed Vernon's hand. "Come on, Vernon," she said. "Come on quick, before John starts home."

Vernon looked at her, startled, but he came.

"Quick, quick!" Edith urged. She was remembering Alena's warning about stories. "Your papa need not be concerned 'bout this," Edith said.

"HELLO, EDIE. How was your first day at school?" Alena said. She was sitting on the daybed, nursing the baby.

"Fine," Edith said. "Just fine."

Alena looked at her closely. "Did you feel . . . well all day?"

"Uh-huh," Edith said. She searched for something to tell Alena. "I have a friend named Rosa," she said.

"Do you now? That's nice," said Alena. She was changing the baby from one breast to the other. The baby did not want to stop sucking even for a moment. She fussed until Alena guided her mouth to the nipple. Alena rearranged her shawl to cover her bare shoulder. "You're sure you didn't feel ill?"

Edith shook her head. She tried to remember feeling ill, but she couldn't. She had felt happy once she got over the strangeness. She had liked school.

"Well then, change your dress," Alena said. "Where is Vernon?"

Edith's heart skipped a beat. "Changing his clothes," she said, not looking at Alena. She slipped her pinafore off her shoulders.

Alena sounded surprised. "Without even being told?" she said. "My goodness, what's got into him?"

Edith blushed and swallowed hard. "I . . . I told him to," she stammered truthfully and was startled when Alena laughed.

"I do believe you're a good influence, Edie," she said.

12
Old Crooked Horn

IT WAS only a little while later that Edith and Vernon were climbing over the orchard fence. Vernon's puppy scooted beneath the bottom rail.

"Are there any cows?" Edith said. "Do you see any cows?"

"Naw, they're all up at the barn. It's getting on to milking time."

Edith searched the shadows beneath the trees. She didn't see any cows.

"Come on," Vernon said. "This was *your* idea."

"We need to hang them somewhere to dry," Edith had told him when they had finished rinsing his school trousers and his drawers in the stream behind the plum thicket. "Somewhere where folks don't go."

Vernon had stared at her blankly. "There ain't no place where folks don't go," he said.

Edith frowned and thought. "What about the orchard?" she said. "The apples are all picked. No one goes to the orchard except to pick apples."

"I go to the orchard," Vernon said. "I like to climb the trees."

Edith glared at him, exasperated. "It can be a place *you* go," she said. "Just not the grown-ups."

"I could climb up high and hang them in a tree," Vernon said, his face lightening. "No one would see them there, not in the back of the orchard."

Edith nodded, smiling. "That's right," she said. "High, high up where the breezes blow. You can get them down again tomorrow when they're dry."

She had not remembered the cows until they were at the fence.

"Come on," said Vernon. "Come on, slowpoke."

It was easy enough for Vernon to climb over fences and up apple trees, even burdened with his dripping trousers, Edith thought. *He* didn't have to be careful of skirts and petticoats. She hiked up her frock and swung her leg over the fence rail. I'm helping *him*, she thought, feeling injured. He should be *nice* to me.

But Vernon was already scampering between the rows of trees, his puppy nipping at his heels. "Over here, Edie," he called. "I know a good tree."

Edith hopped down from the fence and followed him, keeping a sharp lookout for cows.

The tree Vernon had chosen was taller and older than most of the orchard trees. It stood at the far end of a row, slightly out of line with the others. Edith stood beneath it with the puppy and watched Vernon climb.

"That's high enough," she called. The branches of the tree shook dangerously. An apple, missed by the pickers, hurtled through the air, bounced at her feet, and rolled away through the grass. The puppy pounced after it, yapping.

The leaves of the apple tree rustled loudly. The

rustling was all around Edith—above her head as she craned her neck to watch Vernon hang his trousers over a limb, in front of her where the puppy was worrying the apple, behind her in the grass. . . .

Behind her, Edith heard something coming through the grass. She could hear the shuffle of its feet. She could hear the snuffle of its breath. Edith whirled. She looked into the rolling yellowed eyes of a cow.

She screamed.

She ran.

"Climb a tree," Vernon shouted. "Edie, climb a tree."

But though Edith searched wildly for a tree to climb, their branches all seemed above her reach. Their trunks flashed by her as she ran. Beneath her feet, the uneven ground was perilous with fallen branches and clumps of grass and cowpies. Edith stumbled and slipped and ran, her breathing ragged and harsh in her ears. Behind her thudded the cow's heavy hooves. She thought she could feel its hot breath on her neck. She thought its sharp horns grazed her back. She ran.

Ahead was the fence. Edith was sobbing, her tears and breath and the pounding of her heart all one choking thing. She dived beneath the lowest rail and rolled.

Edith was crying. Her eyes were squinched shut, and her arms were over her head protecting it. Little by little, she became aware of the solid ground beneath her. Little by little, she felt the late afternoon sun on her back and began to hear the twittering of the birds. She lowered her arms and peeked at the fence.

The cow stood on the other side of the fence regarding her sullenly.

Edith sat up. She sniffled and wiped her nose on her sleeve.

The cow swung its great black head back and forth. It lowed and pawed the grass with one sharp hoof. Edith saw it had only one horn, and that one was oddly askew. Probably twisted it butting someone, Edith thought. Her heart had slowed with her breathing. She felt irked and sore. The cow snorted, as though in disgust, and turned from the fence. It flicked its tail as it ambled away through the trees.

Edith scrambled to her feet and surveyed her grass-stained frock and mucky shoes. This was what came of trying to help Vernon, she thought. *Now* what could she tell Alena and John? Not that she had been in the orchard hanging up Vernon's wet pants!

She heard the puppy barking.

"Edie, Edie, are you hurt?" Vernon was running along the fence toward her. His face looked frightened.

"I'm not hurt," Edith said. "I reckon I'm not hurt."

"Lordy, Lordy!" Vernon said, gasping as he climbed over the fence. "Lordy, you ran fast, Edie. I didn't think a *girl* could run so fast!"

Edith scowled, but she could feel her anger soften a little. "You said there weren't any cows," she said.

"I didn't think there was. Honest, I didn't. And anyways, most of 'em wouldn't hurt a flea. But when I saw it was Ol' Crooked Horn, I thought you was a goner!"

Edith scuffed her shoes in the grass, trying to rub off the dung. She felt her face go pink. Old Crooked Horn, she thought. I outran Old Crooked Horn.

And then she caught sight of the grass stains on her frock. "Now *I'm* gonna get a lickin'," she said.

"No you won't, Edie," Vernon said. "Not when we tell 'em what happened."

"When we tell them we went to the orchard to hide *your* wet trousers?" Edith said.

"Oh," Vernon said, his voice suddenly quiet. He looked at the ground.

Edith sighed. She pulled up her stockings.

"Well," said Vernon, sounding choked. "Well, we'll just *have* to tell. I can't let you get a lickin' when you was tryin' to help me."

Edith's eyes opened wide, and she looked at Vernon.

His face was red, but his mouth looked determined, and his fists were clenched at his sides. "Come on," he said. "We'd best go in. It's almost suppertime."

Edith watched Vernon walk away from her, the puppy trailing behind. She looked at Vernon's thin, straight back and at his high-held head. "Wait," she called, beginning to run after him. "Wait for me." She was panting when she caught up to him, and her words came between gasps. "We don't . . . have to tell . . . everything," she said. "Say we went . . . to the orchard . . . to play. . . . That's enough."

Vernon glanced at her, and his face broke into a grin. He grabbed her hand. "Come on, Edie," he said. "We're gonna be late for supper if'n we don't scoot."

13
Friends

AFTER SCHOOL on Wednesday, Edith was struggling with the buttons of her apron, but she was not
thinking about changing her clothes. Her eyes kept

going to the empty wooden crate at the foot of the daybed.

"Edie, I need some help," called Alena from the kitchen.

"Coming," Edith said. She hitched up the apron bib so she could reach the top button, then looked again at the crate. The button slipped through the hole. She reached behind to fasten the one at her waist. "I'll be there in a minute, 'Lena," she called, but instead of running to the kitchen when the buttoning was done, she dropped to her knees and poked her head beneath the quilt, which hung over the edge of the bed. Reaching far back into the corner under the daybed, Edith began pulling out her things. Here was her afghan with dust balls clinging to it. Here were her toys. Here was Mother's basket, its tasseled top askew. And here was Pansy Violet Rosebud.

"Bring your dolly to school Friday," Rosa had told her at recess today. "We're going to have a tea party for our dolls to celebrate the end of our first week in school."

"I don't have a doll," Edith had said, not able to meet Rosa's eyes.

"Don't you?" Rosa said. "Oh. Well, then, you can share mine. Her name is Persephone Murgatroid, and she has a china head with black wavy painted-on hair. It's all right, Edith, if you haven't got a doll. Persephone will love having two mamas at the tea party."

Now Edith sat on the floor beside the daybed and looked and looked at Pansy Violet Rosebud. She was a little dusty, and her pink frock was crumpled, but she was just as beautiful as Edith remembered. Edith couldn't imagine a doll more beautiful, not even a doll with a china head and black painted-on hair. Edith untied Pansy's bonnet strings and smoothed her soft yarn hair. Alena had done the ironing yesterday, but Edith felt certain she would help press Pansy's frock, if Edith asked nicely. Then Pansy would be tidy for the tea party, day after tomorrow. I *could* have my own doll, Edith thought. Not just a shared one. She thought she could still feel the warm pressure of Rosa's hand on hers. It was nice of Rosa to offer to share. Still . . . my own doll, Edith thought.

"Lay not up for yourselves treasures. . . ."

It was as though Edith could hear Grandma Malcolm's voice and feel her eyes fixed sharply on her. Edith bit her lip. It was hard to get her breath. Pansy Violet was still smiling—as if she *could* go to a tea party, Edith thought. Edith's fingers felt fumbly and thick as she tied Pansy's bonnet back on. She laid the doll's face down on the afghan so she didn't have to look at the senseless smile. She folded the afghan around the doll and shoved the bundle roughly back under the bed. Thrusting the toys and the basket after, she scrambled to her feet.

"Edie, are you coming or aren't you?" came Alena's exasperated voice.

"I'm coming. I'm coming," Edith cried and ran through the doorway and down the hall as though she were being chased.

THE FIRST THING Edith saw when she opened her eyes was Rosa's face—Rosa's open mouth and horror-stricken eyes. Rosa, looking down at her.

And then she heard John's voice. "Back to your seats, pupils!" he commanded. "Back to your seats this instant!"

Edith was not sure whether the buzzing in her ears was caused by the pain in her head or by the children whispering. She heard the scuffling of their shoes and the creaking of the wooden desks. She heard somebody snicker.

She could not look at Rosa as she pulled herself up and into her seat. A gaping well of sickness had opened at her center. She could feel herself sinking into it.

It had happened, just as Alena had said that it

would. Only Thursday of the first week of school, and already she had had a fit!

"We will continue," John said. "Pupils in the third reader will come to the front of the room to recite. First and second readers may study their alphabets. The rest of you have, I believe, assignments in Barnes's *History*. Edith, you may put your head down on your desk for a moment."

Edith hid her face in the cradle of her arms. There was a hard, heavy lump of tears in her throat.

I will not cry, she told herself. I will *not* cry! She kept her eyes tightly closed, her face turned away from Rosa. I will not cry. I will *not!* she vowed, and her head pounded, fits fits fits!

She must have slept. The pounding was not so strong when she again knew where she was. She could hear voices, one after the other, stumbling through a reading lesson. Listening hard, she was certain she could hear whispers, too.

They had no business to laugh at her! Edith felt her heart speed as her indignation gathered force. I can't help it, she thought. I don't *mean* for it to happen. It's not my fault!

She lifted her head and glared at the children around her. The boy across the aisle was intent upon his book. His finger moved along the line of print, and his lips moved with it. Edith looked at Rosa, and Rosa looked up from her slate.

Rosa's eyes were scared and sad. "Do you feel sick?" Her lips silently formed the words.

Edith frowned and shook her head. She saw Rosa put out her hand, as if to touch her, and she shrank from the touch. She shook her head again, hard, and stared at her own slate. Then she took up her slate pencil and started writing her letters as carefully as her strangely clumsy hand would let her. *A-a, B-b, C-c, D-d, E-e* . . . *E* for Edith, Edith thought. *E-D-* But she didn't know what came next. *F-f, G-g,* Edith wrote, pressing the pencil hard against the slate until it squealed.

"Class dismissed," John said, and Edith felt the relief of it. Now she could go home. Home to Alena. And she would never, never, never come to school again!

Rosa was standing up very slowly. She was packing her book and her pencil and slate into her satchel very, very slowly. Edith wished she would hurry. She, Edith, was going to sit right here until everyone was gone. That way, they wouldn't have a chance to laugh at her.

"Edith," she heard Rosa say, but she kept her face turned away and didn't answer. "Edith," Rosa said, and her voice sounded small and scared.

"Hey, Edie!" Vernon said. He was edging his way up the aisle against the stream of children flowing toward the door. "You done it again," Vernon said. "Right out of the blue! Does your head hurt much?"

"No," fibbed Edith. "I'm fine. Let's go."

"What happened to you, Edith?" said Rosa, sounding frightened. "What happened to her, Vernon? Is she all right?"

"Sure, she's all right. Just had a fit," said Vernon, and Edith wanted to jump up and put her hand over his mouth. But she didn't. She sat, unable to move, her body weighted to the seat. "She has 'em all the time," said Vernon. "Ain't they somethin' to see?"

"All the time?" said Rosa.

"Well, ever' oncet in a while," said Vernon. "Don'tcha, Edie?"

"Vernon," Edith said. "Let's go home!" She grabbed at Vernon's arm. "Come *on!*" she said.

Edith didn't wait for Vernon. She almost ran to the door.

"Idi-it! Had a fit! Had a fit! Idi-it!" The jeers struck Edith like blows as she stepped onto the porch.

She whirled to run, but her way was blocked by Vernon and Rosa following at her heels.

"Idi-it! Idi-it!" mocked the voices from the schoolyard.

Edith could not see who was shouting at her. Her eyes were blurred by tears, and pain leapt behind them, searing and fierce.

They had no right!

I can't help it, Edith cried inside herself. She clenched her teeth against the pain and remembered what John had said. "She is perfectly intelligent." Edith lifted her head, glaring blindly before her. I am *not* an idiot, she thought.

Her hand felt for the railing, and she started down the steps, stumbling a little but keeping her head high. They shan't laugh at me, she thought. I won't let them!

"Leave her alone," she heard Vernon saying. "You leave her alone, or I'll tell my father!"

"Idi-et and teacher's pet!" a voice cried, and the others shouted with laughter.

Edith felt Vernon step beside her. He was walking with her down the steps.

"Go away!" yelled Rosa. "You leave us alone and go away!" Rosa was running down the steps. She took Edith's hand.

"What are you doing, fellas?" said a new voice.

Edith wiped her sleeve across her eyes. One of the biggest boys, one of the boys who rode the blaze-faced mare to school, was trotting over astride his horse.

"Can't you find someone your own size to pick on?" the big boy said. "You such sissies you got to plague little kids?"

The boys who had been taunting them were moving away, their calico-shirted shoulders hunched. Edith saw through her tears how they scowled. "Aw, we was just havin' a little fun," one boy said.

The big boy on the mare looked down at Edith and Vernon and Rosa, who stood at the foot of the steps. "You want me to ride a ways with you?" he asked.

Edith looked at him. His face was kindly. He was not laughing at her.

"No," she said shakily. "No, that's all right. Vernon and I walk together."

"I don't think they'll bother you again," said the big boy, "but if they do, you just give a holler. I'll take care of 'em." He dug his heels into the mare's smooth brown sides.

Edith watched as he rode away.

She could feel Rosa's hand, warm in hers. "Meanies!" Rosa said, and Edith saw she was crying, too.

"Bullies!" Vernon said, his face red. "Big ol'

bullies! Snot-nosed bullies! Lordy-Hell-fire-and-Damnation!"

"Vernon!" Edith said. She put her hand quickly over his mouth and glanced in the direction of the schoolhouse door. "Your papa'll kill you if'n he hears!"

Vernon clamped his mouth shut and kicked at the bottom step. "Damnation, Damnation, Damnation!" he muttered under his breath.

Rosa giggled. She let go Edith's hand and covered her mouth, but the giggles slipped hysterically between her fingers.

"Shhh!" Edith hissed. She grabbed Rosa's hand away from her mouth. She grabbed Vernon's hand and ran.

The breeze of their running dried Edith's face. It cleared the pain from her head. She gasped the cleansing breeze into her lungs.

Edith and Vernon and Rosa tore across the schoolyard to the black-oak tree. They fell upon the ground.

"Oh, oh," Edith giggled. "Oh, did you see those bad boys slink away?"

"Cowards," Vernon said, a smile lighting his eyes. "They're just big cowards, that's all."

"That Ivan Hadley is a nice boy," Rosa said.

Edith looked from Rosa's tear-streaked face to

Vernon's. "So are you," she said. "You are a nice girl, and Vernon is a nice boy, too."

Vernon and Rosa looked uncomfortable. Rosa sat up and straightened her frock. Vernon began to tuck in his shirt.

"Thank you," said Edith. "Thank you for sticking up for me."

"You're my friend," said Rosa.

Vernon grinned. "And you're my *aunt*," he said.

14

A Big Girl

ONCE again their voices kept Edith awake.

"And you didn't bring her home? John!" Alena cried. Edith could hear the dismay in her voice.

"She was perfectly recovered in just a few minutes," said John. "It is as I said. The seizures pass quickly and do no permanent harm."

"And the other children? How did they react?"

"They were, of course, disconcerted," John said. "They will become accustomed in time."

Alena made a noise. Edith could not tell whether it was a laugh or a cry or something else altogether.

"They will torment her," Alena said after a little. "They will make her life unbearable."

Edith pulled herself up in bed and leaned her head against the wall. She clutched Alena's quilt to her throat.

She heard John say, "She has already shown herself equal to that."

"What do you mean?"

"After school some boys were calling her names. She ignored them. She walked right toward them and held her head high. Edith has more sand than you give her credit for."

Alena's voice was outraged. "You did not stop them?"

"I did not need to. She had her defenders. I am proud to say Vernon showed himself loyal, and little Rosa Aebischer and the Hadley boy both spoke up for her. I watched through the window, but there was, as I anticipated, no need to interfere."

Edith caught her breath in surprise. In the darkness, her eyes grew round. John had been watching through the window this afternoon! Edith did not know whether to be angry or glad.

She could hear Alena's footsteps pacing back and forth across the room. A board creaked whenever Alena trod on it. Pad, pad, pad went Alena's bare feet. Pad, pad, creak, pad, pad. It was an agitated sound.

When John spoke again, it was in his firm, loud, *final* voice. "Edith must continue to go to school, Alena," he said. "She is quick to learn, and today she showed the stuff of which she is made. She was facing them down, Alena."

"But why should she have to?" It was a cry. "She is only a child, John. Only a little girl. And she cannot help her . . . spells. Why should she be made to suffer still more?"

John sounded as though he were reading a lesson. "What is important, Alena, is not that Edith has these seizures, but that she gets up again! She does not need you or me to pick her up. She can do it for herself."

Again Edith heard the strangled laugh-cry sound Alena made.

But I *do* need 'Lena to help me, Edith thought. She could feel the self-pitying tears welling in her eyes.

Alena's voice, low and determined and coldly

angry, shocked Edith's tears away. "Edith is *my* sister, John. She shall not return to school. I shall send her home to Faith and Will."

"No!" Edith said aloud. "No, no!"

I must go to school, she was thinking. I haven't learned to read yet, and tomorrow is the tea party. I *have* to go to school. . . . But . . . home to Faithie and Will and the boys? Edith tried to imagine it. Home to her high chair with the cut-off legs, to her cot up under the eaves? But I'm a big girl now, Edith thought. I sleep in the baby's room and keep her from being afraid. I sit in a big chair, and pretty soon I won't need the dictionary. With Faith and William and the boys, Edith was the baby. But here . . . here I am Vernon's aunt, Edith thought. Here *I* am the biggest girl.

She was out of bed, her feet cold on the floor. She was feeling her way to the door.

I don't want to go home to Faithie and Will, thumped her heart. I want to go to school.

The door opened. Her heart had been beating so loudly she had not heard them coming.

"I *have* to go to school," she cried. She flung herself at Alena, and the tears started flowing. "I have to," she said. "Don't make me go back to Faithie and Will. I want to stay here!" Edith clung hard around Alena's neck. She cried so loudly she could not hear what Alena was murmuring. "I want to go to school," she cried.

"And so you shall," said John, his loud voice cutting through her sobs. "You shall go to school, and you shall stay with us."

Alena was holding Edith tightly in her arms.

"Don't coddle the child!" John commanded. "Put her back to bed, and come to bed yourself." He was talking to Alena, and then suddenly he was talking to Edith, too. "It is time to go to sleep, Edith. No more listening through walls, do you hear? You should be ashamed!"

Edith snuffled and hung her head.

John turned away. "Are you coming, Alena?" he said as he went.

Alena carried Edith to the daybed. She helped her crawl under the quilt and tucked it under her chin. Alena's tears, warm and wet, were falling on Edith. Edith could hear her shuddering breaths.

"I want to stay here," Edith said in a very small voice. "I want to go to school."

Alena's voice was a sigh. "Hush, hush," she said. "I know. Hush, hush."

Alena kissed Edith and straightened up. She went to the crib and tucked in the sleeping baby.

" 'Lena?" Edith could see Alena's white night-gowned shape and the pale bars of the crib. "Can I, 'Lena? Can I?"

Alena walked to the doorway. She stepped into the hall and pulled the door closed after her. Just before it shut, Edith heard her whisper, "Yes."

EDITH was up early on Friday. She washed her face and brushed her hair and did up her buttons herself. Then she knelt beside the daybed and pulled out the Chinese basket and the toys and the rose-colored afghan bundle. She opened the basket on her lap.

The Testament lay on top. Edith picked it up and riffled through the soft pages until she found the dried pansy. When she lifted the pansy from the page, it left a stain, the faintest browning of the page in a pansy shape.

Lilies of the field, Edith thought suddenly. That was in the Bible! Lilies of the field, rose of Sharon, cedars of Lebanon . . . all that was in the Bible. Why, even God loves pretty things! Edith thought.

The pansy was fragile in Edith's fingers. She turned it in the morning light. Its gold was faded almost to brown. Its purple was pale mauve. And still it was beautiful because . . . because Mother loved it, Edith thought. Because it was a treasure.

Perhaps I was mistaken, Edith thought. Perhaps . . . perhaps treasures have nothing to do with fits. . . . Alena says fits are just something that happen to me, something I can't help. But . . .

But I can get up again! John says *I* have sand! Edith thought.

She laid the pansy carefully back between the pages of Mother's Testament. *My* Testament now, Edith thought. She took out the ribbon coil and the little gold brooch. Then she leaned over and put the basket and the Testament into the wooden crate at the foot of the bed.

The crate looked nice, Edith thought. There would be something in it even when she took out her shoes.

Edith scrambled up and hauled the chair over to the chest of drawers. There was a small mirror over the chest into which she could just see when she stood on the chair on her tiptoes. Edith let the ribbon unfurl, a shining streak of blue. She pulled her braids over one shoulder and tied them together with the ribbon. She pinned her collar with the brooch. She thought she looked quite grown-up.

Edith climbed back down off the chair and looked at the afghan bundle. Laying up treasures?

she thought, testing the thought for danger. Then she straightened her shoulders and picked up the afghan from the floor.

Pansy Violet Rosebud was very rumpled. Edith shook her head. There was not time now to press her frock.

"You'll just have to go to the party as you are, Pansy Violet Rosebud," Edith said. She sighed and tried to smooth the frock with her hands.

Pansy smiled at her. She looked glad, and not at all ashamed of her wrinkled frock.

Edith settled Pansy on the chair and began to spread up the daybed. She smoothed the sheets and the sky blue quilt, then took up her afghan and shook it out. She laid it over the quilt. She fluffed her pillow and put it in place, and then she stepped back.

Her daybed was rosy and cozy, Edith thought. Her wooden crate was full. She picked up Pansy Violet Rosebud and gave her a hug. The sun shone warmly through the window lighting Pansy's smile.

15
The Joy We Share

THE RAIN had come in the night, changing almost imperceptibly from heavy dewfall to this cold steady drizzle. It made getting to church on Sunday a drippy business, though it had not rained long enough or hard enough to mire the roads.

John halted the surrey before the church steps while the family climbed down. "Mind the puddles,

Vernon," he ordered and watched until Vernon was safely in the vestibule.

Edith picked her way around the puddles, careful without being told of her freshly shined shoes. She followed Grandpa Malcolm and Vernon down the aisle and into their pew. Hands primly folded in her blue plaid lap, she tried to sit still and straight, but she could not keep her eyes from following each new arrival down the aisle. She saw Faith and the boys come in, and she saw Rosa, holding the hand of a lady in green. Rosa grinned when she caught sight of Edith, and Edith felt the grin all through her like a hug.

Grandpa Malcolm bulked large at one end of their pew, his beard and hair exactly the color of his iron-gray suit. John installed himself at the other end next to Alena when he had tied the horse.

"You must help me if the baby fusses," Alena whispered to Edith, leaning toward her over the baby's basket, which was on the seat between them. She handed Edith a sugar tit, a spoonful of sugar tied in a clean square of cloth. "You may give her this," Alena said.

But Edith did not think the baby was likely to fuss. Her eyelids kept fluttering open and closed in a half-hearted effort to stay awake.

The organ wheezed to the end of the prelude as

the choir filed in. The pastor stepped to the pulpit. The people shifted and sighed. The service began.

Outside the tall, narrow windows of the church, the rain misted down with a soft, sighing sound. Inside, bracketed lanterns made pools of light in the grayness. Edith breathed the warm smell of damp leather and wool, of pipe tobacco and eau de cologne and kerosene. The people almost snuggle, she thought as they rose to sing the first hymn.

Edith's mind wandered as announcements were read. She thought of the first week of school just past, and she thought of Rosa, her friend. She thought of Old Crooked Horn and of their race, and she smiled now remembering her fright. She thought of the secret of Vernon's wet trousers. She thought of the tea party on Friday at school.

When Edith closed her eyes, she could shut out the voice of the pastor, telling about the deacons' meeting next week. In her mind, she could hear instead Rosa's small delighted gasp when she, Edith, had pulled Pansy Violet Rosebud from beneath her pinafore Friday morning. "Why, Edith!" Rosa had said. "You do too have a doll. May I see?" And Edith had held Rosa's Persephone while Rosa examined Pansy from bonnet to shoes. Persephone Murgatroid was a pretty enough doll, a store-bought doll with an elegant silk-faille frock. Still, Edith knew that Pansy was better. Persephone was hard and shiny and cold, and Edith was glad to hug Pansy's rag body when Rosa handed her back.

They had had to put the dolls away then, high on the cloakroom shelf to wait until lunch recess. Edith could scarcely stay in her seat that morning. Her letters danced a jig on her slate; her eyes kept leaping to meet Rosa's; her heart kept jumping for joy.

And it seemed to Edith, when lunchtime *finally* came, that she had never been so happy. So . . . just like all the other girls, she thought as she sat in their circle beneath the black-oak tree. She passed the sugar bread Alena had sent, and giggled when the other girls giggled, and met their friendly eyes with her own. And she kept her little finger crooked just so as she pretended to drink tea—which was really well water—from the tiny china cups that Rosa had brought. . . .

Now in church Edith came to with a start. Alena was touching her arm with the collection plate. Edith had a penny, given her by John, to drop into it. The penny clunked in the felt-lined plate with a satisfying sound. And then the pastor was inviting John and Alena forward for the baby's baptism.

Alena lifted the baby out of the basket, arrang-

ing the long skirt of the baby's gown so it fell grace-
fully over her arm. Edith watched her walk up the
aisle beside John. The whole congregation was
watching, she thought, seeing how handsome they
were. John stood so tall, his pomaded head high.
Alena was wearing a feather-trimmed hat. They
faced Pastor Rost on the walnut-railed platform.

The pastor smiled as he began the ritual:
" 'Hear the words of our Lord Jesus Christ. . . .' "

Edith could not see the baby in Alena's arms,
but she could see the snowy folds of the long baptis-
mal gown. Alena had said that once she, Edith, had
worn that gown. And Vernon had, too, and Chester
and the other boys. "Our mother made it for our
family," Alena had said. "All our babies wear it."
Edith had fingered the lace at its hem. "You were a
beautiful baby, wearing our family gown," Alena
had said.

"Vernon, too?"

Vernon had blushed. "Not me," he said.

But Alena had said, "Yes, Vernon, too. Vernon
looked beautiful, too."

"Let us pray," the pastor said.

Edith bowed her head and tried to listen and
join in the prayer.

"May we be made one with Christ our Lord in
common faith and purpose," the pastor said.

When the prayer was finished, the congregation stood and spoke an affirmation. Then the pastor was saying, "What is your child's name?"

And John answered in a loud, clear voice. "Letitia Mary Malcolm," he said.

Edith said the name to herself in a whisper. "Letitia Mary." Mary was Edith's name, too. Edith Mary. And Mary had been Mother's name. Mary Elizabeth. The names felt durable on Edith's lips. Family names.

"Letitia Mary Malcolm," the pastor was saying, "I baptize you in the name of the Father and of the Son and of the Holy Spirit. Amen."

Edith saw him dip his fingers into the font and sprinkle the drops of water from his fingertips onto the baby. She heard the baby gasp and saw her arch in Alena's arms. She could picture how the baby must be screwing her eyes shut and opening her mouth wide, how her face must be growing red. She was not surprised when she heard the baby's high-pitched shriek.

The congregation laughed.

Alena put the baby against her shoulder and patted her back. The baby cried, and the pastor waited, beaming. John looked discomfited, Edith thought, but the pastor seemed ready to laugh. At last there was quiet enough for him to say, "This child of God is now received into the holy Catholic church. See what love the Father has given us, that we should be called children of God!"

Another prayer, the baby snuffling against Alena's shoulder, and then the pastor was shaking John's hand and patting the baby's head.

Edith was waiting with the sugar tit when John and Alena came back to the pew. She popped it into the baby's mouth when Alena had settled her into the basket. Edith stroked the silky fuzz of the baby's hair. The lantern light above them gilded the faint down that edged the curve of the baby's ear. It seemed to Edith the blue veins of the baby's temple throbbed with the beating of Edith's own heart.

"Letitia Mary," Edith whispered. Letitia-Mary-Edith-Mary-Mary-Elizabeth.

THEY STOOD on the porch of the church, waiting for John to bring the surrey around. A wagon drove by with Faith beside William on the seat holding an umbrella over their heads. The boys huddled in back. They grinned and waved, and Edith and Vernon and Alena waved back.

Edith watched the wagon lurch away down the puddled road. Many a Sunday since she had come to live with John and Alena, she had wished she could go home with Faith and Will and the boys. Many a Sunday, her heart had been heavy watching them drive away.

But this Sunday, Edith felt a smile on her face as she waved good-bye. The memory of Faith's hug and William's teasing voice were still with her. I will see them again next Sunday, she thought. And next Sunday and next Sunday and next Sunday. And sometimes Faith will come to help 'Lena and me, and sometimes we will go to help her. And next summer, there'll be a nice long visit, Faith had promised. "You can come stay for a time, you and Vernon. You and the boys can have a good romp."

Edith thought that would be fun—to be with the boys—though Chester seemed so much grown of a sudden. He had treated her like a baby today, calling her Little Sis.

And then Edith's thoughts were interrupted by the arrival of the surrey, and she was climbing into it. "I can do it myself," she said when Grandpa Malcolm started to lift her up.

E D I T H was beginning to feel hungry. She snuggled beneath Grandpa Malcolm's greatcoat and tried to remember if she had seen Alena dressing a hen for dinner. Her mouth watered at the thought of crisp roast chicken and stuffing with sage.

"Wouldn't have missed that for all the world," Grandpa Malcolm was chuckling. "She's got a lusty yell, our gal. Made Widow Brown sit right up to listen, I'll tell you. She'd nodded off—I saw her head go down—but when Lettie let loose, her head jerked up. Didn't go back to sleep the whole danged service. I'll vow that's the first sermon she's heard these twenty years!" He slapped his knee, and Edith and Vernon laughed, snuggled against his sides.

"Father Malcolm!" Alena chided, but Edith saw her smile.

The rain was now a steady downpour. The side curtains did not keep it entirely off, and the going was heavier as the road grew more bogged. John's hands holding the reins looked strong and tense.

Edith saw Alena take the baby from the basket and hold her under her cloak. The baby had begun to cry, and Edith wondered if she were hungry, too.

The return trip would be long, Edith knew, but she felt safe and warm beneath Grandpa Malcolm's big arm. She settled into the jolting rhythm of the surrey as it carried her toward home.

ON SUNDAYS they used Grandma Malcolm's silver, which had come, she liked to tell them, from
the fine big house in town where she grew up.
Grandma Malcolm did not like Edith to touch the
silver, but today John overruled her. "It would be a
help to Alena," he said. "Edith knows how to place
the silver."

Edith did know. Alena had taught her how to
put the fork on the left and the knife on the right,
blade toward the plate, with the spoon beside it,
when she set the table with the everyday ware.

Importantly, Edith carried the correct number
of silver forks to the table. Vernon gets mixed up
about right and left, she thought, but I don't.

When she returned to the kitchen to get the
knives, Vernon was telling Grandma Malcolm the
story of the baby and sleepy Widow Brown. "You
ought to have seen it, Grandma," he said.

Grandma Malcolm's eyes looked angry. Perhaps she doesn't believe him, Edith thought. "I saw
it," Edith said. "Her head jerked right up like she
was stuck with a pin."

Vernon laughed. "Best thing that happened all
morning," he said, "except for sprinkling the baby.
That's what made her cry, you know."

Grandma Malcolm shelled peas into a pan on her lap, her knotted little fingers jerking at the pods. She did not laugh. Not angry, Edith thought. *Sad.* Her eyes are sad because she couldn't see it herself.

"Most babies cry at baptism," Grandma Malcolm said. "You cried when you were baptized."

"Not me," Vernon said and looked at Edith. "Maybe Edie did."

"You both did," Grandma Malcolm said shortly, and Edith felt suddenly sorry that Grandma Malcolm was old and ill and smelly.

Vernon pouted, kicking his stockinged foot at the leg of the stove.

Edith began to count out the knives. Vernon and I were both baptized, she thought, and we both cried. And 'Lena probably shushed us like she shushed Baby Lettie. She imagined herself a little baby rocked in Alena's arms . . . or was it Mother's arms? They were all mixed up in her mind. It was a long time ago, she thought.

Edith looked up from the spoons at Vernon's sullen face and felt sorry for him, too. "You can carry these to the table, if you like," she said, thrusting the silver knives toward him. "You know how to put them around on the other side from the forks."

Vernon took the knives. " 'Course I do," he said, and Edith saw how his face lighted up.

"I'll count out the spoons," Edith said.

The rain swished against the windows. Baby Lettie fussed. Grandma Malcolm's rocker creaked. As Alena basted the chicken, the juices sizzled in the pan. Outside the door, John and Grandpa Malcolm stamped the mud from their feet.

One-two-three-four-five-six, and a little one for Lettie. Edith counted out the spoons, one for each member of her family. She began to hum, and the humming changed into words, "*And the joy we share as we tarry there, None other has ever known.*"

AFTERWORD

EPILEPSY, the chronic disease of the nervous system that caused Edith's seizures, is one of the oldest recorded diseases. Hippocrates wrote about it in the middle of the fifth century B.C.

In England, in the 1860's, potassium bromide was discovered to have some effect in controlling seizures, but its use was not widely practiced, especially in rural areas. Even at the end of the nineteenth century, many doctors knew very little about it. It was not until 1912 in Germany that barbiturates were found to be effective. Most epileptics of Edith's time, the late 1800's, simply had to learn to live with their seizures as a fact of their lives.

Today, epileptic seizures can usually be controlled with medication, and most epileptics lead normal lives.